Also by Alex S. Reid,

Reid's Short Reads,
Glimpses of Fun and Fear

MORE REID'S SHORT STORIES

Glimpses of funny, weird and wacky folk.

ALEX S. REID

authorHOUSE®

AuthorHouse™
1663 Liberty Drive
Bloomington, IN 47403
www.authorhouse.com
Phone: 1-800-839-8640

Illustrated by Arianna Palmer and Rand Darrow

This is a work of fiction. All of the characters, names, incidents, organizations, and dialogue in this novel are either the products of the author's imagination or are used fictitiously.

Published by AuthorHouse   07/21/2014

ISBN: 978-1-4969-2405-6 (sc)
ISBN: 978-1-4969-2404-9 (e)

Library of Congress Control Number: 2014911971

In my search for an illustrator I contacted the art teacher at my local High School. Arianna Palmer was thrilled with the opportunity to be part of this book. Rand Darrow, both illustrator and author of Witches, Wolves and Water Spirits, also helped. Thank you.

CONTENTS

CAMEL RIDE ROMANCE

S ARAH, THOUGH LONG SINCE RETIRED, was still an attractive divorce'. She took great pride in her appearance and looked twenty years younger than she actually was. Her figure was trim, her dress sense neat and stylish. She was fun, intelligent and a delightful, incurable romantic.

This explains why the camel driver she had met while on her recent vacation to Egypt didn't just look like Omar Sharif, to her, *he was Omar Sharif.*

Typically, Sarah's evenings were spent alone, curled up with a romantic novel. Later she studied travel brochures, then dream of exotic far-off lands.

I first met Sarah at a neighbor's barbecue. She was fresh from her, 'once in a lifetime trip' to Egypt. Her words bubbled as she described the Sphinx, the pyramids, the olive groves, endless desert, *and her handsome camel driver.* After a few glasses of wine her tongue loosened, her cheeks flushed, as we learned of Ahmed.

"I was standing with a tour group of seniors when Ahmed first noticed me," Sarah began.

"Our eyes met, he smiled, and I felt my heart leap as he walked over. We chatted as I admired his striking, dark good looks. He invited me to join him that evening for a camel ride by the Nile. How could I refuse?" she whispered shyly, her eyelashes fluttering like a teenage girl about to share a deep dark secret. "We met that evening after dinner. His teeth glistened like ivory in the soft moonlight spilling over the Great Pyramid," she continued, warming to her fantasy.

"His turban and white linen robes fluttered, almost glowing in that warm, magnificent night. Ahmed commanded his camel to squat before he reached down and helped me climb up behind him. My arms wrapped tightly around him as I inhaled the sensuous, musky mix of Ahmed and his camel," she continued, gesturing with one hand, her other shaking while sipping on her glass of red Chianti.

"The swaying palm trees, and the slow, rhythmic walk of his camel had a strange, heady, hypnotic effect on me," she said, her eyes now glazed.

"The moonlight," she continued, "along with the warm, scented breeze drifting across the Nile was intoxicating, romantic, and relaxing. We bobbed along so slowly and gracefully that I was afraid I might doze and fall off. I pulled closer to Ahmed, grabbing more tightly onto his saddle horn. Ahmed turned and smiled, his scarf brushing my cheek. No doubt he sensed my excitement and was aware of how this magical night was affecting me. He rarely spoke as I pressed closer, my head resting on his muscular back," Sarah continued in short whispered breaths, her eyes shining, reliving her unforgettable experience.

"Suddenly, his legs stiffened as his camel trotted faster, then into a slow gallop. I was nervous, so I gripped more firmly onto his saddle horn. He dropped his reins and raised his arms sideways like wings. Moments later he threw back his head and wailed as if he were in pain. I'll never forget his long, piercing cry into that star-strewn Egyptian sky. His scream sent the river's bird fowl scattering before rising high into the night sky as the goat herder's dogs began barking. It was all too much for Ahmed. He probably was as overwhelmed as I, by the magic of the night and it's perfumed, intoxicating breeze," Sarah said, her cheeks now flushed, pausing to hold out her glass for more Chianti.

"How wonderful," we all gushed, the guys grinning and elbowing each other as the ladies wriggled, whispered and giggled.

Most of us knew that saddle horns were used by American cowboys for roping steers. It was therefore most unlikely that the saddle on Ahmed's camel had a horn.

CLYDE'S SECRET

C LYDE WAS BIG. NOT ONLY six feet three tall, but weighed two hundred and eighty pounds with broad shoulders and huge hands. He was a bit of a mamma's boy with girlish mannerisms. We noticed the little things. The way he stood with a hand on his hip, or his holding his coffee cup with his pinky sticking out.

He was in his mid forties with always neat, wavy, silver gray hair. He was heavy on the cologne which made most guys uncomfortable. His dress sense was flashy. One day he wore a Western style black shirt with white fancy stitching on the shoulders and pearl buttons. His matching pants, white belt and cowboy boots were too much.

"Jeez Clyde where's the friggin' square dance?" someone hollered across the office. We teased him a lot. He was easy to pick on because he was shy and good natured. Though he rarely got angry, I managed to get to him a few times. One time while he was describing an incident when he was in boot camp in the army, I interrupted, "You were in the military? Which outfit, the Pink Berets?"

Clyde jumped up and pressed his face close to mine. "One of these days . . ." he threatened, holding a huge fist inches beneath my nose. We knew that he was joking even before he smiled and plodded back to his desk.

In spite of all our kidding we knew there was nothing truly swishy about Clyde. Many times we'd caught him checking out the good looking girls around the office.

His home life was no picnic because his wife was something of a nightmare. Though little more than five feet tall she was Sicilian and had a violent temper.

"When she's mad she throws things," he confided.

"What kind of things?" we asked.

"You name it, chairs, dishes, knives," Clyde said. "One time a full bottle of Chianti."

"Knives?" I repeated, in disbelief.

"Yeah. A butcher's knife. It stuck in the kitchen door. Lucky I ducked . . ."

We laughed, but guessed there was truth to his stories. Though long married, Clyde never spoke of children.

He was plagued by problems with the neighborhood kids. They'd ride their bikes back and forth outside his home, yelling and tossing empty soda bottles onto his front lawn. He'd holler, threatening to call the cops and they'd leave, then wait to see if cops came. When they didn't, the kids returned and the circus began again.

In summer he had a new blacktop driveway installed.

'Don't drive on it for a week until it hardens,' the contractor warned before driving away with his heavy equipment. Clyde placed large, orange, vinyl cones at the end of his driveway by the road. The neighborhood boys watched with interest. Minutes later when Clyde glanced through his front window his orange cones and the local boys were gone.

"Okay you little bastards, that's it," he said while dialing for the sheriff. Fifteen minutes later the sheriff's car pulled into his driveway . . . *then sank up to its hubcaps.*

While working at adjacent desks we discussed everyday things. I had mentioned wallpapering our daughter's bedroom.

"My wife wants me to wallpaper our downstairs bathroom. I've bought the paper and was planning on doing it next week while she's visiting her family in the Bronx, Bronx," Clyde said.

"Ever wallpapered before?" I asked.

"No, but how hard can it be?" he said.

"Well, let's just say that bathrooms are the very worst. Cutting around cabinets, vanities and tiling are pretty tricky. What kind of paper did you buy?"

"Jeez, I dunno. Vinyl pre-pasted?" he said.

"That's not good . . . the paste dries fast while you're still cutting. It'll probably peel off while your wife's taking a shower. Then I'll read about her knocking you off in a rage. Tell you what. You spring for pizza and sub-sandwiches and I'll wallpaper your bathroom for free. How's Monday and Tuesday of next week?"

The wallpapering went pretty smooth, though it was Wednesday night before I finished. Clyde offered to help, but his bathroom was too small for both of us.

"Thanks a million," he said when it was finished. "It looks great." He stood with one hand resting on his hip while offering me a cold beer.

"Jeez Clyde. Any idea what you look like?" I said flicking a thumb toward his hip.

"Sorry," he said, smiling.

I cleaned up the paper trimmings, gathered my tools and loaded my car. Clyde mopped the bathroom floor, then returned his stepladder to the garage.

"Before you leave I'd like you to hear something," he said. I followed him into his formal lounge. So far I'd only seen his kitchen and bathroom. I slipped off my shoes and felt my stocking feet sink into the lush deep pile of his white carpet. A log-fire flickered in the fieldstone fireplace which reached to the ceiling. Rich, burgundy, velvet drapes hung from tall windows on three walls. A Japanese cabinet inlaid with mother of pearl and ivory figures filled half of one wall. Beside it was a low coffee table with cut-glass crystal decanters of wine and liqueurs resting on an engraved silver tray.

In the center of the room was a magnificent concert-sized grand piano. Its finish was so black, polished, and shiny that the reflection of the fireplace's flames danced on one side.

"That piano's been in my family for over a hundred years. My grandfather was a concert pianist. He brought it over from Europe," Clyde said.

"Do you like classical?" he asked, while sitting, then cracking his knuckles and beginning to play before I could answer.

I pulled a high-backed, carved oaken chair closer and placed a magazine on it, aware of the wallpaper paste on my pants.

Clyde's music was soft and light at first, then it grew louder. He played from memory, flawlessly and with confidence. I recognized the piece but couldn't name it.

"Chopin?" I offered when he had finished.

"Very good," he said, and then began another. I marveled as his large fingers danced over those keys. I thought of all the teasing he'd taken. He had laughed, rarely getting angry. We'd mocked him, ridiculed him, and said cruel, unkind things. Through all of it the joke had been on us. Because Clyde had known what we had not. That he was blessed with a special gift for music. A rare, precious talent which flowed within him.

I closed my eyes to savor his music. It was strange and haunting. It took me back to a time of my childhood, when I was ten, hiking with my granddad in Scotland's highlands.

"Ever watched the eagles fly?" granddad asked as we climbed ever higher above the loch? "It's a rare, bonny sight that you'll nay forget," he had said.

Sheep grazed everywhere on the coarse grass among the scattered granite rocks. The mist rolled down those heather covered mountains. We rested on a crag high above the valley. Three hundred feet below, the River Doon snaked like molten silver through the valley. We ate our sandwiches and drank tea from a thermos.

There they were. Four golden eagles swooping, falling and crying, playing high on the winds sweeping upward through those jagged cliffs.

Clyde's playing affected me as no music ever has before or since. I knew that I was experiencing something unique and I was humbled.

"That was amazing," I said when he stopped playing and I opened my eyes.

"You could play in concerts," I said.

"I'm not even close," he said. "My dad was a soldier. He and my mom met during the war at a village dance. They planned to marry but he was shipped overseas in 1944 and died in France. Mom was pregnant with me. She was pretty messed up emotionally. I guess she'd wanted a girl. I found baby pictures of me after she died. She kept me in dresses until I was five. Mom was a music teacher. As a kid all I ever knew was piano lessons. I never had the chance to play baseball or run in the streets like other kids. I hated the piano but she wouldn't let me quit. I cried while practicing for two hours every night. Eventually practice became such a part of my life that I still do it, even now."

"It wasn't a waste Clyde. You have great talent," I said.

"Thanks again for the bathroom," he said. "When my wife gets back we'll all go out for dinner, my treat."

"Great. My wife will love to hear you play."

"Deal," he said. "But please don't tell the guys in the office that I play piano."

"I promise," I said.

I've kept my promise for over thirty years. Recently I read Clyde's obituary in the local paper. He'll no longer mind my sharing his secret.

Now, whenever I close my eyes and think of him, I can still hear him playing. I imagine he's entertaining the angels. They'll enjoy his music just as much as we did.

CONSPIRACY THEORY

"EVER WONDER IF THERE'S A School of Aggravation?" Chuck asked, his left eye twitching.

"A School of Aggravation? What's that? " Iggy asked.

"It's where people go to learn how to *really aggravate people*. They learn new ways to push us over the edge," Chuck said.

Chuck and Iggy met every Wednesday in Joe's diner for a late breakfast. They'd been friends for years and now retired, had time to discuss world problems. Chuck the thinker, was tall bald and skinny. He wore a red flannel shirt and blue jeans held up by suspenders and a belt. Thick glasses and bushy eyebrows framed brown beady eyes which rarely glanced from the diner's front door.

Iggy was quick humored and easy going and had a mischievous grin. He wore a brown Carhartt jacket and a farmer's cap pushed back on his head. A mop of long white hair hung below his cap atop his red, chubby face. He slouched, relaxed, leaning sideways against the corner of their booth. He was the less-talkative one, feigning interest in Chuck's problems and enjoying his endless banter.

"Why'd anyone want to aggravate us?" Iggy asked, winding up his friend.

"Isn't it obvious? It's a right wing conspiracy. Hillary recognized it years ago. Remember all the lies they spread about poor Bill?"

"I tried phoning you yesterday but couldn't get through," Iggy said, changing the subject.

"That's 'cause I had it disconnected."

"Why'd you do that?" Iggy asked.

"'Cause, each time I sat on the john, my phone rang. Complaining to the guy at the phone company was a complete waste of time. Can you believe it; he laughed. The dumb ass said I should check with my psychiatrist? What would my shrink know about telephones?" Chuck said.

"I sent you an E-mail, but it was returned," Iggy continued.

"That's 'cause my computer had a malicious virus," Chuck said. "Damned thing was screwing up my home's electronics."

"How'd it do that?" Iggy asked.

"You're asking me? Don't get me started. My toast jumps out of my toaster too soon. My remote garage door-opener didn't work. Then a mile up the road my car's trunk pops open. Last week my sump pump quit and my basement flooded. But right after I dropped my computer, my electronic problems miraculously went away."

"You dropped your computer off your desk?" Iggy asked.

"No, out my office window," Chuck explained.

"Even my local supermarket's joined the aggravation movement. Yesterday I stopped by for a few things. Two women stood chatting. Naturally their shopping carts blocked the aisle so I couldn't get by. I stood for a while waiting patiently, thinking they'd see me and move their carts. But no, of course not," Chuck continued.

'Excuse me,' I said politely. They turned and glared as if I was making an unreasonable request. Nearby, a pathetic guy was bending over, peering at a shelf of canned beans, talking on his cell, 'The beans dear . . . should I buy Heinz or Grandma Browns?' I felt like asking, 'Jeez fellah, make a decision! You're not buying a damned house.'

Chuck stopped talking, glanced nervously around, and then placed an index finger to his lips. "Shhh," he whispered, pausing as the waitress came over to top up their coffee.

"She listens," he explained after she'd left.

"Then we have zombie drivers," Chuck continued. "Let's not talk about *those* nitwits. Does anyone use turn signals anymore? Yesterday, I'm perched on top a twenty-foot ladder cleaning leaves from my gutters. Some idiot drove by and beeped. What was that? Was I supposed to wave and risk breaking my neck? I didn't know who it was . . . and still don't. Let's face it, people are annoying," Chuck said.

"I took my wife to a nice restaurant for dinner. Do you think we might enjoy a quiet, pleasant conversation? Of course not. From nearby we have a woman's screeching, singing voice that'd shatter glass. Next we are treated to America's latest musical delight . . . rap music. . God help us," Chuck groaned.

"And aggravating people aren't just here in the States. Hell no. They've invaded Europe. In the seventies my company shipped me to Scotland for two years. Those Scots have raised aggravation to a real science."

"How'd they do that," Iggy asked.

"Well, for starters, their miserable weather gives 'em a huge advantage. During our first year there it rained twice . . . from January 'til late October . . ."

"C'mon Chuck, you're exaggerating. *It couldn't be that bad.*"

"Bad? It was bloody torture. Then we had the bagpipes . . . like banshees . . . wailing, morning, noon and night.

My Company sent me over there to improve the plant's Quality Control. Do you think the Scots wanted my help? Of course not. Their Commie union's shop steward hated me from the start. First he threatened to call a strike, and then get me fired.

Then, would you believe, every electrical appliance we bought was defective?"

"In which way," Iggy asked.

"In every bloody way. Listen, I'm not making this stuff up. We bought a steam iron. There was no plug on the power cord so I had to buy one and install it myself."

'My steam iron has no hole where I pour in the water,' my wife complained.

'Of course there is," I insisted, in disbelief. 'Read the instructions?'

'I did, but there's no hole,' she said.

'That's not possible,' I said, then checked for myself. She was right, *there was no hole.*

We bought an electric toaster. Again, no power plug. After adding a plug, we dropped two slices of bread in the toaster. Two inches of each slice stuck out above it and never got toasted. I'm talking about *regular sized bread.* Only a graduate of Aggravation University would design such a dumb thing.

Would you believe that none of the *appliances we bought had a power plug.* Washer, dryer, vacuum cleaner, lamp, drill, hair dryer, none of them. Why? Because homes in Britain have a variety *of different electric wall receptacles.*

Then we had the wallpaper incident. After wallpapering three walls of our bedroom, we opened the remaining rolls. They were different from the first ones. The part numbers matched but the colors didn't.

One Friday lunchtime, I drove to the local bank to cash my paycheck. A single line of customers stretched from outside the bank's door to the teller's window.

'Are you the only teller?' I asked, after waiting twenty minutes.

'Yes, the other tellers are at lunch,' the lady explained. For the bank's manager to leave just one teller during the bank's busiest time was pure brilliance. Tell me that he wasn't an Aggie U. graduate," Chuck said, catching a breath, then continuing.

"Why would mothers with babies in strollers all bank during lunchtime? Wasn't their whole day free? Aggravation. U., graduates? They had to be.

That same lunch hour, I was hungry and stopped at a sandwich shop. There were two lines of customers. I joined the shorter one. Behind the counter was a variety of freshly made sandwiches. On reaching the counter, I asked the sales lady for a ham and cheese sandwich.

'Sorry luv,' this line's for bread. That other line's for sandwiches,' she said sweetly.

'But the sandwiches are on the shelf behind you. Can't you pass me one?" I pleaded.

'*I could,* but that wouldn't be fair to our other customers, now would it sir?'

I skipped lunch that day," Chuck said.

Just then a loud, throbbing sound passed over the diner, interrupting their conversation.

"What's that noise?" Iggy asked.

"A helicopter . . . it's probably tracking my car. They use 'em whenever their spy satellites are down," Chuck explained.

"How could they recognize *your car?*" Iggy asked.

"They've numerous ways. This morning I noticed fake wild goose crap on my car's roof. There were bright green, dots and dashes . . . probably Morse code. I fooled 'em by shuffling those marks around." Chuck explained, beaming proudly.

"You've gotta be making this stuff up," Iggy said, grinning widely, revealing the gap in his front teeth.

"Oh yeah. Have you tried opening pill bottles lately? Drug companies spend thousands designing bottle caps that senior citizens can't open. They claim it's to protect children, but we all know that's a crock. When my eight year-old grandson sees me struggling with my pill bottle, he pops it open like nothin'"

"That's true," Iggy said. "But there're worse things.

"Like what?"

"Like the weird, stupid names people give their kids, like Orville, Jasper, and Alfonzo," Iggy said.

"Like, 'Iggy,' right?" Chuck said, grinning.

"It's short for Igor," Iggy said. A common name in Eastern Europe where my dad's from. You're lucky having a name like Chuck . . . short for Charles, right?" said Iggy.

"Hell no! It's short for Chuzzlewit. Ever heard of Charles' Dickens' *Martin Chuzzlewit?* Can you believe that my old man read that book in school and liked the sound of it? He stuck me with that stupid name, the sick bastard. Right from early childhood, I never stood a chance. High school was pure hell. It's a miracle I'm normal" Chuck said, his voice down to a whisper.

"Wow, smell that chili? Iggy asked, changing the subject quickly so that he wouldn't laugh.

"Chili's your favorite . . . right Chuck?"

"It used to be," Chuck said, in a low, sad tone. "But no more. Not since they started loading it with mushrooms."

"When did they start doing that?" Iggy asked.

"A week after our waitress heard me tellin' you I hated mushrooms. I'm tellin' you Iggy . . . *they are all out to get me.*"

DAMNED CAT

IN THE MID 1930's, LIFE for Mac and Moira in their coal-miner's village, high in the Scottish highlands, was tough. Each evening when Mac came home, his back ached from swinging a pick and shovel at the coalface. His skin was stained black from thirty years of sweating in the coal dust which he inhaled with each breath. Each night he bathed in a wooden tub, the water heated in the cauldron hanging over the coal fire which burned all year. Mac's wife Moira scrubbed his back, so often bruised from falling coal. She then rinsed his once red, now white hair. When they first were married, it was as wild and thick as a lion's mane. How life had changed since their four children moved away. They sometimes wrote, but seldom visited for there was little time for travel. Work chewed up their lives and swallowed it in great chunks.

It was a six-mile bike ride from the pithead to Mac's cottage. As he pedaled, he continuously coughed up thick, black phlegm. Most miners walked, but he'd saved, and then bought the bike which he now leaned against his cottage wall. By habit, he peeped through his kitchen window. There it was. That damned ginger tomcat, as always, asleep in his brown easy chair by the fireplace. God how he hated that ugly cat with its half-chewed ear, and the droopy eyelid from an old fight. Even worse, was its persistent peeing on the side of his chair.

Tomcats do that to mark their territory. With his chair close to the fireplace, it reeked. Mac would scrub it with laundry soap, and next day, the cat sprayed again. Mac had lost track of the number of times he'd come home and tried grabbing it. But the instant the kitchen door creaked open, the cat was under the cupboard. Jabbing it with a broom didn't help because it was too quick. The saga had continued for years. Ever busy, the unsmiling Moira didn't help, because she liked the cat. It was a good mouser, and her fear of mice far outweighed the aggravation. Mac's efforts to get rid of the cat was a longstanding family joke. Moira had long since decided the cat was smarter than her husband.

"You're strong in the arm, but weak in the 'ead," she teased whenever the cat outwitted him, which was often. But sadly, she realized that the red cat offered color to their drab lives.

Dirty grey clouds hung like shrouds above the village. They were polluted by the belching smoke from two hundred stone cottages. Tall hills, almost mountains, trapped the dark clouds which blocked sun and sky but not the rains. They always got through. When the heavy lashing rains rolled down the grey-green hills, they quickly filled the streams which then gushed into the River Doon which writhed, snake-like through the valley. It rained often, mostly in steady showers of cold, fine, coal-dust drizzle. When they began, the miner's wives scurried outside to bring in their washing before it was wet and dirty.

On dry days, their washing hung as limp as dead fish, for there was little wind. The granite walls and slate roofs of the cottages were blackened from the soot of eighty years. Behind their simple homes lay patches of small vegetable gardens. The miners planted mostly potatoes, onions, carrots, and beets, having learned that with so little sunshine, root vegetables were their only hope.

One mid-August day, the strong winds, high above the valley, swept the heavy, gray clouds away. It was rare for an evening to be sunny and warm. Now home from the mine, Mac wheeled his bike down his garden path. He spotted his ginger cat lying asleep on the shed roof. He froze and leaned his bike against his cottage wall. The cat didn't move as he crept closer, and lifted a potato sack from off the fence. He slipped two bricks in the sack, and then grabbed the now struggling cat.

"At last I've got you," Mac said grinning while stuffing the cat into the sack and securing it with cord as the cat growled and clawed wildly. He hung the kicking sack over his bike's handlebars as he coasted down the brae for fifteen-minutes to the lower valley. He stopped on the stone bridge arching over the barge canal, and tossed the sack over the wall. He paused, listening for the splash which never came. Instead there was a dull thud.

"What the hell . . ." he said aloud, before climbing off his bike and peering over the wall. Below him, the burlap bag lay jumping and wriggling on a heap of heavy black sacks. They were piled on the back of a coal barge now passing slowly beneath the bridge. A man walked slowly ahead, leading a dray horse which clomped steadily along the canal's towpath while pulling the thirty-foot barge.

"The damned cat has the luck of the devil. What're the odds? Mac wheezed open-mouthed. He watched in disbelief as the barge glided slowly and steadily onward, to the foundry, ten miles away. *'The barge master'll hear the cat's cries and let him go. Then some other family'll adopt him and he'll make their lives miserable,* 'he muttered.

"Well, good riddance," Mac said, talking to himself, then tamping tobacco in his pipe, lighting it, and puffing contentedly. He stood leaning on the bridge wall, savoring the sight of the man, horse, and barge, moving steadily away. He felt the beginnings of peace and freedom from the torment of that damned cat.

While pedaling slowly home, he planned his evening. He'd celebrate with a beer with supper, then he'd scrub his chair for the last time to get rid of the stink. Finally, he'd soak his tired muscles in a hot soapy bath. If Moira were to complain of mice, he'd buy her a tupenny trap.

He leaned his bike against the cottage wall, then by habit, glanced through the kitchen window. His heart jumped, as an icy chill ran down his spine and his face paled.

"Sweet mother of god," he spluttered, "It's come back to haunt me."

There it was, curled up, sleeping peacefully in his chair by the fire.

"The bloody thing's in league with the devil," he said aloud.

Minutes passed before he dared step through his door. Moira saw his expression of disbelief. She stood, leaning forward, her hands on her knees, laughing hysterically, barely able to talk.

"You daft bugger. You grabbed our cat's brother . . . our neighbor's cat," Moira said.

Miners are superstitious folk. When you escape a close brush with death, you are believed to be under heaven's protection. Mac never troubled his cat again.

It lived for seven more uneventful years before dying peacefully, asleep by the fireplace, in Mac's smelly, old brown chair.

DOG WHISPERER

IT WAS A STEAMY HOT mid-summer day in Florida, when Angus made his first visit to Pavloff's Veterinary Clinic. He'd heard that this vet was known as a Dog Whisperer; an animal shrink who could help with your pet's emotional problems. Many scoffed at such things but Angus believed that animals are just as likely as humans to be confused.

After completing the questionnaire, giving his address, dog's name, breed, etc., he chose a corner spot in the waiting room. Rascal sat on his lap so both could watch the other pets and their owners.

"Doctor Pavloffs running late," the receptionist announced. Angus didn't mind. He enjoyed watching folk reading magazines or fiddling with I-Pods. Many pet owners have few human friends, preferring instead the company of animals. Angus didn't think that *he* belonged *in that* category. He had many friends. Well two, one being his brother. Angus was in his late thirties, quiet, single, and something of a loner. He was contented with just the company of his pup.

Rascal, his Cairn terrier, wasn't sick, not health-wise anyway. He'd had all his shots, was big for three months, and was still at the playful stage. Rascal's problem was confusion. *He believed he was a cat.* There was a good explanation for this, and Angus knew what it was.

It began the night Angus heard a mouse in his kitchen. He didn't like mice so he decided to get a cat. Days later he noticed a, 'Kittens Free' sign on the old ladies' mailbox across the street. He stopped by and met the old lady along with her eight cats. She gestured to a litter of three kittens with a puppy playing with them on the kitchen floor.

'Take your pick,' she said. The mother cat lay sleeping in a large wicker basket. Angus recognized the puppy immediately as a Cairn terrier. Evidently the old lady thought the puppy was a kitten. Angus didn't tell her because he knew that a purebred Cairn terrier was worth major bucks. 'If the old girl thinks it's a cat, so be it. Why tell her and drive up the price?' Angus reasoned.

"I'd like this one," he said picking up the puppy and hugging him closely.

'Someone left him wrapped in an old sweater on the front porch,' the old lady explained.

'He was so cold and weak I didn't think he'd make. I gave him to Gertie who already had three kittens. She accepted him as one of her own. Gertie's a wonderful mom. I named him Rascal, because he gets into mischief.'

Though rare for a cat to adopt a puppy, Angus had heard of such things. He felt a twinge of guilt and offered the old lady twenty bucks. She took it. 'Win, win,' Angus muttered to himself while carrying Rascal home. The name suited the little guy so Angus kept it.

In the Vet's waiting room across from where Angus sat was a tall, loud mouthed, bottle blond, heavy woman in a pink pants suit. She was chomping steadily on doughnuts from a paper bag on her lap. Beside her leg was a white, fancy sculptured French Poodle. To Angus' left was a man who was less than five feet tall. He wore a neatly pressed tailored suit and a cheap hairpiece. He had a firm grip on a short heavy chain leash on which was a black, mean looking pit-bull.

The waiting room door swung open and a fourteen-year-old boy crept through. He clutched a fishbowl close to his chest. A large fan-tailed goldfish swam around inside. The fish was swimming upside down.

"It started a week ago," the boy explained to the receptionist.

"My dad says it has Labyrinthitis. Some call it 'swimmers ear.' Dad knows, 'cause he had it one time. It's caused by fluid in the inner ear. It's messed-up my fish's balance," the boy explained. Swimmin' upside down doesn't seem to bother him, I think he likes it."

Just then, a tall, well dressed lady walked in carrying an empty parrot cage. After giving her name, the lady sat by the window and placed the cage on the floor beside her. Everyone stared at her empty cage wondering what happened to her parrot.

"It's an African Gray," the lady explained to her audience, all puzzled by her empty cage.

"African Gray's make the best talkers. *Whitney* here prefers to sing. She listens all day to the radio." Moments later the unmistakable high-pitched voice, amazingly like *Whitney Huston's* arose from that empty cage, 'I . . . will always love you . . .' The lady's lips moved slightly and her throat muscles trembled. Either the lady was an accomplished ventriloquist or she had an invisible parrot.

"I hate that damned song," the short man with the bad hair piece announced to the whole room.

"Everywhere I go they play it. Restaurants, stores, even my car radio. It's torture," he said in a loud, nasal, whiny annoying voice.

"Relax," the big blond said. "It's just a bird. Keep your hair on."

"Keep my hair on! What's that supposed to mean?" said the short guy with the bad hair.

"I'm sorry," said the blond. "It's just an expression. I didn't mean your wig."

"My what?"

"Your rug. Look, I wasn't being rude. Obviously you're overly sensitive, being you're so short and all."

The parrot began singing again, "Iiiiii . . . wweeeel . . . alllwaaaays . . . loooove . . . yooooo. ."

"Quiet Goliath," the parrot lady said, tapping on her empty cage. By then it had already stopped singing.

"Goliath? You're kidding right? Who'd give a parrot a giant's name for gosh sakes," the short man said.

"Now he doesn't like giants. I wonder why?" said the big blonde, chuckling.

"I'm not too crazy about fancy French, pansy-assed, dogs like yours either."

21

"That's 'cause you drug dealers prefer pit bulls, am I right?" said the blonde.

"So now I'm a drug dealer. Honestly lady, for a fat, ugly woman, you really know how to hurt a guy."

At the peak of their awful, heated exchange, the receptionist announced, "Mr. Shorthouse, the doctor will see Butch now."

"Lord help us, did she say, Shorthouse?" asked the blonde lady laughing hysterically.

"That's beautiful. It ought to be short-ass. Now I get the attitude."

By now Angus had had more than enough. He needed to escape from this zoo and find another veterinary dog shrink someplace. He'd never met such a bunch of weirdos.

There had been a recent rain shower but it was still a hot, stifling afternoon, even for Florida. As Angus carried Rascal across the steaming parking lot, a young girl saw them and waved. She walked over to Angus' car just as was lowering his car windows for cooler air, and placing Rascal on the passenger seat. The young girl stood by Rascal's window and asked if she might pet him.

"Sure," Angus said. "He's very friendly."

"What's your cat's name?" the girl asked, reaching inside the window.

"His names Rascal, but he's a dog," Angus said, a little irritated.

The girl gave Angus a puzzled look before nervously stroking Rascal. When Rascal's back arched, his tail stood vertical and he began purring loudly, any doubts which the girl may have had, disappeared. She pulled her hand from the car window.

"Thank you," she called nervously over her shoulder while scurrying back to the safety of her family, waiting patiently in their car.

ENGINEERING
APPRENTICE SCHOOL

I WAS ONE OF TWENTY-TWO, fifteen-year-old boys, fresh out of school and beginning an adventure. A six-year long, engineering apprenticeship in Trafford Park, Manchester, England. We were from nearby cities and small towns, thrown together to manage as best we could. We were a mix of tall, short, thin, and fat lads. Most were quiet, well-behaved, nice kids. Others were rough, and rowdy street-smart kids who'd steal your lunch, your toolbox, even your shirt if given the chance. Our language soon became rough, peppered with obscenities.

We learned cuss words we'd never heard before. Some of us were the dregs of English society, the dropouts, often forgotten by their families. At eleven, we had all failed the nationwide, 'Eleven plus Exam.' It deemed us not bright enough to attend High School and too young to join the military.

In this sad, odd mix of society's rejects, bonds formed, friendships grew, and teams were made. There was humor, pranks and constant laughter as twenty-two rookie apprentices pounded on chisels from Monday to Friday, eight hours each day for four weeks. The cacophony of clanging steel rang through the workshop. Our energy was focused on a two-inch diameter, one and a quarter inch long, mild steel bar. Our objective was to produce a test piece, a perfectly square cube. A micrometer ensured its accuracy to within plus or minus five thousandths of an inch. We used a hacksaw, various chisels and files, a ball-peen hammer and emery cloth. The chisel was our greatest problem. After many hours of pounding, its head became rounded. The hammer would then skid off our chisel and thumb knuckles were whacked, bruised, and bloody. Our screams and cusses rang out constantly through that simulated factory floor. Peals of laughter would follow because one boy's pain was a great source of humor for others.

We wore steel-toed safety boots and navy-blue boiler suits with pockets everywhere. One pocket was long and narrow and stretched down the outside of our right thigh. Its purpose was to hold an eighteen-inch long steel rule. As none of us had such a rule, we found a much better use for the pocket.

As one apprentice chiseled diligently on his steel block clamped tightly in the vise on his workbench, another boy would stroll casually along the aisle behind him. Pausing for a second, the passerby would slip the neck of a funnel into his victim's rule pocket, and then continue walking. As the unsuspecting victim continued filing away, another boy walked past, stopping just long enough to pour a can of cold water into the funnel, gently remove it, and then move on. Minutes later the cold water had soaked through his pants and began trickling down his leg. He'd then begin a comical, wild, high stepping, leg-shaking dance as his shoe filled. Our cheers and screams of laughter never failed to bring our instructor running over to see the cause of the commotion.

"This is a Training School not an asylum you bloody nitwits. What's wrong with you kids?" he'd yell.

Though safety was of high priority, apprentices were often injured. It was a weird and primitive rite of passage.

Albert Singh was a dark skinned Sikh, recently from India. He was a quiet, unsmiling, serious young man. Religion was a solemn and sacred part of his life. His boiler suit was neatly pressed, his turban pure white, and he wore the fluffy beginning of a beard. He was smart, aloof, and rarely spoke. He viewed his fellow apprentices as infidels, lower class, unworthy untouchables.

Curly Elliot, our bald-headed, red-faced instructor, often conducted tours with seven apprentices around various work areas. One day he stopped in the machine shop to explain how the guillotine or shear worked. We used it for cutting steel bars and rods. While demonstrating the shear's operation, Curly, our instructor gripped the four-foot-long handle. As he droned on and on, Singh, bored, stood behind him, staring with fascination at the hole through which steel rods are fed. Ever curious, Singh poked his right index finger into the shear's hole. That very instant, Curly dragged down the handle. Singh screamed, staring in disbelief at the stump of his finger, before fainting onto the workshop floor. The deeply shocked Curly Elliot, assisted by two apprentices, half-carried Singh to the ambulance room.

Curly was now in big trouble and we all felt bad for him. Of course it was pretty dumb of Singh to stick his finger into that hole. Bill Zimmer found Singh's finger under the bench.

"Take it to the ambulance room," someone suggested.

"They might sew it back on," another said, amid laughter.

"You do it," Zimmer snapped. "I'm not touching that thing."

Zimmer finally agreed that as he'd found it, he deserved the credit for it. He knelt, rolled the finger onto his steel rule, and then walked slowly along, careful balancing the finger to the nurse's office. It was an unfortunate coincidence that he met Singh just as he was leaving the nurse. His bandaged hand was held chest-high and Curly was clutching his elbow.

"Hey Singh," Zimmer said cheerfully, thrusting the finger within inches of Singh's nose. "I found your finger." Singh stared for a brief moment before his knees buckled and down he went a second time.

"Jesus Zimmer. What's wrong with you?" Curly yelled.

"What?" Zimmer said." I thought he'd want it."

"I gave Singh the finger," Zimmer explained later. "He was the whitest Indian I've ever seen," he said, trying not to smile.

We never saw Singh again. It was sad because we all liked him. Though frankly, he never cared very much for us.

Art Bates was big, blonde haired, and weird. He was loud, talked incessantly, and had a severe nervous affliction. Every twenty minutes or so his eyes would blink rapidly, his head would jerk up and down three or four times, his jaws snap open and close, and his teeth click loudly together. At that same moment his left hand would flick rapidly waist high, as if shaking hot glue from his fingers. Art had no control of this strange behavior. It may have been Tourette syndrome, unknown back then. Though he was the constant source of attention he made light of it. He even managed to make it funny, probably to avoid embarrassment. He was the most colorful character I've ever met. Art was from Bolton, a bustling Lancashire town known for its textile industry and the unique, broad dialect of its natives. Visitors to Bolton often questioned if the locals were speaking English.

The constant pounding on our chisel's head caused it to become rounded. Art's affliction caused his hammer to skid off his chisel head more often than most. At least six times each day Art hit his thumb knuckle with his hammer. Each time he'd scream, drop his hammer and chisel causing two loud clangs, grab his thumb, and then begin a vigorous high stepping dance. All this, while yelling, "Ah, ah, ah, ah, mang-el-ed," as his jaw snapped noisily, his head bobbed violently and his hand whipped up and down in a blur.

Art's unique painful dance was contagious. We loved it. Now, whenever one of us hit our thumb, we too became Whirling Dervishes. We'd all contracted a weird sickness which our instructors were powerless to cure.

Later, after moving to the blacksmith's shop, we found even more ways of getting injured. Better yet, we discovered new and creative opportunities to sabotage our fellow workmates.

We pounded by the hour on heated steel bars, forging them into horseshoes, screwdrivers, tire-irons, and crowbars. Using various tools, we shaped red-hot steel after first heating it in the hot coals of the furnace. We handled the hot bars with thick leather gloves and long steel tongs. With time we grew careless and overconfident, grabbing the unheated ends with our bare hands.

When a bare-handed victim wasn't looking, we'd switch the steel bar around so that the end he thought was cold was really the hot end, straight from the furnace. The result was an animalistic scream, as our victim hopped around in an impressive, primitive dance, accompanied by our favorite song, "Ah, ah, ah, m-a-n-g-l-e-d." We would all quit hammering on our horseshoes, slap our knees, and howl our appreciation of the circus.

'Mean Dean' was our pale-faced, unsmiling, foul-mouthed Blacksmith Instructor.

He had strong muscular arms and brown crooked teeth. Stubbs, our fellow apprentice was his pet, his favorite, 'bar basher.' This was because, for some strange reason Stubbs made great horseshoes. We never fully understood the need for all our horseshoes because we were training to be Electrical Instrument Makers. Anyhow, Stubbs had a habit of sitting on a low, cast iron table while waiting for his iron bar to heat in the furnace. We would wait for the moment he left his seat to lean forward to check on his steel bar in the hot coals. We'd then slip a very hot, flat steel plate onto his seat. Seconds later Stubbs sat down, then leaped high, before racing, screaming to the bathroom with blue smoke trailing from his rear. Our favorite song, "mang-el-ed," accompanied his comical gallop.

Each apprentice's steel toolbox had a padlock because our tools were precious. Without them we couldn't work, and theft was common. Most of us were still paying for them with weekly deductions from our meager paycheck. A group of trainee College Apprentices worked at nearby benches. We didn't like them for many reasons. Mainly it was because they were richer, smarter, taller, and better-looking. They had posh accents and were four years older than us. Being jealous, we mocked, and picked on them. They all looked as if they'd just stepped from the shower. Their coveralls were crisp, neatly pressed and their black boots new and shiny. Those chaps were all that we were not.

Their toolboxes were big and expensive. Those college guys were careless about locking them when they left for lunch. One day one of our lads took an oil-soaked rag, lit it, stomped out the flames, and then tossed it into a college kid's toolbox. He snapped the lid closed, padlocked it, and then hid the key. Minutes later when its owner returned, he found smoke spewing from every hole in his toolbox. He screamed like a girl while skipping around pouring cold tea over it. Next he sprayed the work area with a fire extinguisher. Meanwhile, black clouds of thick oily smoke continued bellowing from his toolbox as instructors raced over yelling, "Fire, fire." Meanwhile, our unruly bunch of social misfits slapped our thighs, chattering hysterically like chimpanzees.

Dougal was another whacko apprentice. He was only five feet tall, and as hairy and muscular as a monkey. He hated being short and had a bad attitude. He disliked anyone taller than himself, which was everyone. I worked on the bench beside him, well within range of his wrath. He'd insult and cuss at me for the slightest thing, then watch for my reaction. I once tried making friends by offering him a banana from my lunch. It didn't help.

He cursed more than anyone I've ever known. The usual swearwords seemed inadequate so he invented new ones. It was as if the old ones had lost their power. He needed newer, fresher ones to better express himself. The day he called me a 'dog's nostril,' I laughed. I thought him creative and funny. However, laughter wasn't the response Dougal was looking for so he never used that again.

Another time he was mad at me for something, such as my habit of patting him gently on his head as if he were a small child, he called me a 'black melt.' Again I laughed because not only was I not black, I had no idea what 'a melt' was. Sixty years later I still don't.

One day he called me a 'Scotch git.' After much pressing he explained that a 'git' was the offspring of many, many generations of one's forbears never troubling to marry. I laughed again, explaining to Dougal that he was half-right.

"My dad is Scottish which satisfies the Scotch part. Marriage however is very common among my human forebears. But I'm far less familiar with the customs of your 'tree swinging relatives.' " I said.

It's hard to believe that Dougal and I became good friends. He was most upset the day he failed his Driver's Road Test.

"What happened, Dougal?" I asked, feigning interest.

"The Driving Test Examiner was a just a tall, miserable asshole. He failed me for some minor, stupid reason."

"What minor, stupid reason was that?" I asked.

"No consideration for other road users," Dougal said.

"What does that mean?" I asked.

"Oh some minor crap," he said.

"I'd stopped to let an old lady cross the street at a zebra crossing. She must've been ninety, hobbling along with a cane, really slow. I waited, waited, and waited until I couldn't stand it anymore. Finally, I wound down my window, leaned on my horn, and hollered, 'Hurry up, you doddering old bastard,' Douglas said.

"Yep. That would do it," I agreed.

During the year that we spent in the school, we learned the basics of manufacturing. There was mechanical fitting, welding, milling, turning, the drill press, sheet-metal work, armature winding, and electrical instrument making. Each day we attended classes where we learned to read measuring instruments such as Vernier calipers, micrometers, Johanssen Gage Blocks and Brunel hardness scales. We learned to read, and produce engineering drawings, and to write specifications. Using every form of coercion and psychological ploy, our instructors finally succeeded in instilling in each of us a sense of responsibility and pride in our accomplishments. Yes, even respect for safety. We played chess while in daily classes. This helped think, to plan ahead, and exercise logic.

After twelve months, we transferred to the real world of the factory. For the next five years, we moved every six months to different departments to experience areas such as electrical instrument inspection and calibration. Finally I settled in a drawing office designing high voltage switchgear for coalmines and power stations. One day each week plus three evenings we attended courses at a Technical College, all paid for by the company. Though our apprentice's pay wasn't great, our training was recognized worldwide as the finest.

Eventually, after having caused our instructors to tear out their hair and some seek other careers, my 'whacky, dumb, greasy, foul-mouthed, borderline delinquent fellow inmates' blossomed into responsible tradesmen. Even Curly Elliot admitted later that his great surprise was that none of us 'wound up in the clink.'

Today I enjoy retirement after a successful career consulting with the world's finest companies such as, IBM, Xerox, Burroughs, Eastman Kodak, General Electric, Grumman, and Johnson and Johnson. I remain good friends with Alan in Australia, Rob in England, George in South Africa and Harold, who enjoys life on an island in the Philippines. Each of us arose to high management positions within our respective companies.

Looking back, we appreciate that our instructors did a miraculous job. Especially when one considers the weird, rough bunch of social misfits which they were forced to work with.

FAITH HEALER

PERCY HAD A SPEECH IMPEDIMENT and talked funny. Having contracted polio as a child, he now wore steel braces on his legs and needed crutches. Though handicapped, he was always cheerful and had a mischievous sense of humor. He never complained of his misfortune and enjoyed life. Being with him was fun and whenever we felt low, Percy would cheer us up.

We'd heard that a faith healer was coming to town. Stories quickly spread of this healer's miraculous cures. The man credited them to the power of prayer; coupled with his healing prowess. Percy wasn't just skeptical of his powers; he didn't believe any of it.

"It'th all bulthyit," he lisped. "Heeth jutht a fake, looking for thuckerth," he insisted, as we struggled not to grin.

"You should give him a chance, "we all insisted. "What do you have to lose?"

Percy finally agreed to visit him. He travelled alone by bus, as each of us had to work on that day.

The next evening we gathered around Percy in our local pub. We were all anxious to learn of his experience. He sat alone in an alcove beside a flickering coal fire. He was unusually quiet and there was no sign of his crutches.

"What happened, Percy? Tell us all about it," we begged, while dragging our chairs beside him, impatient for news.

He looked up and smiled, thrilled by our great interest.

"There wath about thixsteen people there," he began. "Everyone there had thomething theriouthly wrong with them. The faith healer man wath dressed in a long black robe like a preitht. He theemed

31

pretty old and had a nithe, kind fathe. Thith helped put uth all at eathe," he said.

"Go on . . . go on, we urged impatiently."

"Well, he chothe me firtht. I wath embarrathed when he athked me to thtand up," he continued.

"Then he plathed a hand on my thyoulder and thaid a prayer. I felt really thtrange, like thunthine wath thining on my fathe. Then he reached down and took my right crutch away. My heart thtarted ratheing."

"That's great. What happened next?" we asked excitedly.

"I wath awright," Percy replied.

"Amazing," we said in unison.

"Praise the lord," said another.

"Then what happened?" we asked.

"Then he told me to toth my other crutch away."

"Incredible," we gasped.

"God be praised," someone added."

"What happened next?' we asked.

"What do think happened, you athholes? I fell on my bloody fathe," Percy said, grinning broadly while draining the last of his beer.

LEAVES OF THREE

IT DOESN'T SEEM POSSIBLE THAT a small plant could ruin one's life; yet one did.

My wife and I had recently bought our dream home, way out in the country in upstate New York. Had we listed all that we were looking for in a home, we couldn't have found one more perfect.

It was a hundred and thirty years-old farmhouse standing on three acres of wooded, part swampy land, overgrown with weeds on a patch of meadow. Our three young children loved the place immediately. Our two boys found the spot for a tree house and our daughter Susan chose the stable in the barn for the pony she hoped for.

My wife was thrilled with the spacious country kitchen with its endless cabinets, while I had a three-car garage with space for the workshop I'd always dreamed of. It needed work, but being young, I believed that I could perform miracles. How much I needed to learn.

"Watch out for the Poison Ivy," my neighbor warned.

"What is that?" I asked, innocently, grinning and ignorant of the treacherous weeds.

"Oh boy, welcome to the country. It's a persistent, invasive weed which grows throughout your woods. If you brush against it, you'll have a miserable, itchy rash," he explained.

"What's it look like?" my wife asked. Our neighbor pointed to a few harmless looking plants peeping shyly from beneath the tall ferns growing around the house.

"Ever hear the old warning, 'Leaves of three, leave them be?'" he asked.

"Nope, never did," we replied.

That's how it began. The beginning of a stressful period of our life. One of prolonged, torment and aggravation.

Our children, forever playing outside, were the first to develop red, itchy rashes on their legs. Soon it was on their faces, hands and arms. At night they scratched and clawed at themselves before crying themselves to sleep. We bathed the oozing patches with calamine lotion trying to prevent it spreading. Our children looked as if they had some terrible disease. Often they were too embarrassed to attend school. On those days, my wife stayed home from work with them. We begged friends and our local pharmacist for advice on treatment, but as fast as we cleared one outbreak, another began. We tried numerous soaps, Fells Naphtha laundry soap being our favorite.

We learned that urishial oil, the plant's poisonous leafy sap, caused the itchy rash.

When something comes in contact with the oil, it remains active for years, awaiting someone to touch it. The gray-white seeds of the plant are a favorite winter food for birds and small animals. Later the plants are spread from their droppings. Our wild animal neighbors seemed in league with this invasive plant. We lived in a country paradise, near a delightful small town in apple country, close to Lake Ontario, yet felt threatened. Not by something we could readily deal with, but with an elusive enemy which tormented us. It hid, disguised as a harmless weed lurking among our daffodils and wild flowers.

After Sammy, our dog, chased squirrels in the woods, his fur would bring the oil into our home. Onto our sofa, chairs or carpet, the oil, awaited us. When our cat clambered up my ladder to our barn's loft in search of mice, her fur brushed the ladder's rungs. The next time I climbed up there, my hands and fingers became affected.

Everything which our cat or dog brushed against became contaminated. It seemed impossible to avoid the terrible plant. It was essential that we shower within a half hour of coming into contact with the plant and all our clothes thrown into the laundry.

By the end of our first summer, we knew that Poison Ivy had declared war on us. We were plagued by an enemy which attacked us both in our woods and our home. It lurked silently in the shadows beneath our trees and tall weeds. Poison Ivy creeps along the ground among innocent ground covers such as pachysandra, periwinkle and violets. It imitates English and Boston ivy by climbing vine-like up the trunks of the trees among the wild grapes. If poison ivy vines are burned, fine particles of its oil hitch rides on the wind, invading our clothing, skin, and our lungs.

Once we knew we were at war, we questioned ever buying our home. But by fall, the magnificent deep crimson, orange and purple of our Maples and Sumac, and the gold of our Quaking Aspen and Ash dispelled our doubts. One special evening as my wife and I stood watching a breathtaking sunset, we smiled, knowing we could never leave this place.

In spring, as the first signs of poison ivy begin reaching up from the fallen leaves, I began spraying. I vowed to search every square yard, then find and kill each hateful plant and vine. Each morning I arose at first light, mixed and filled my pressure spray canister and headed out, bending, and spraying throughout my woods. An hour later I'd strip off my clothes, toss them in the washer, shower, dress, and then head to work. I repeated this every day, all summer long, rain or shine. Even then, there was always one member of our family with an itchy rash.

We could no longer pet our dog Sammy. Whenever we stepped outside, we wore gloves; even in summer.

My wife became concerned with my emotional state and sought advice from our family doctor.

'I noticed my husband's strange obsessive compulsive behavior in late summer,' she explained to him.

'His nightmare incident really scared me,' she said.

'Nightmare incident? 'the doctor asked.

'Yes. He awoke from a deep sleep, snapped on the light, then leaped out of bed, yelling and pointing at the wall paper. His eyes were wide with terror,' my wife said.

'Look,' he yelled. 'It's right here in our bedroom. Poison Ivy's now climbing up our bedroom walls!'

'I tried explaining that it was the grape-vine design on our wallpaper,' my wife said. 'We chose it together before wall-papering our bedroom the previous spring.'

'But he wouldn't listen. Instead he leaped up, grabbed his gloves, a scraper and then began feverishly scraping, and ripping off huge strips of the wallpaper. Our children were crying and terrified. None of us had any more sleep that night. Other nights were almost as bad,' she said, pausing to wipe her eyes. She continued in a lower voice. 'One time he awoke in the dark early morning, mumbling about new plants growing in the woods. He dressed quickly in his old work clothes and chest-high fishing waders, grabbed a flashlight and headed out to the barn. I watched through our kitchen window as he mixed the spray before tramping into the woods. I tried reasoning with him but he wouldn't listen.

When he began threatening to get rid of our dog Sammy because the Poison ivy was using him as a weapon against us, I knew we needed your help doctor,' she said, her voice close to breaking.

'Clearly, your husband needs a psychiatrist,' her doctor advised. 'I'm afraid that he's beyond the scope of <u>my</u> expertise,' he added.

Extensive tests showed that my behavior had reached the stage necessary for my admittance to a special care facility for round the clock surveillance.

Weeks later my wife met with my psychiatric care doctor.

'My colleagues have examined your husband and determined that he's suffering from a rare, but advanced case of Botanophobia; the fear of plants,' the psychiatrist explained.

'His initial response to therapy, rest, medication and isolation was excellent. In fact far better than we'd hoped,' he explained. 'But then, we had an unfortunate incident which caused his severe relapse,' he paused, searching for the right words, uncomfortable with the topic. Nurse, Krystyna Ivanowski was assigned to him. Your husband and nurse Ivanowski quickly became friends. Then, for no apparent reason, your husband's behavior changed dramatically. He became uncooperative, erratic, and even violent. It required that we increase the dosage of his medication. Our nursing staff had difficulty spelling and pronouncing nurse Krystyna Ivanowski's name.

Please believe me when I assure you that had they been aware of your husband's medical history, they would never have begun calling her, ***Nurse Ivy.'***

MIDNIGHT FLOWERS

O N A WARM MID-AUGUST NIGHT in 1918, after their local pub closed, Fred and Annie took a walk. They decided on a moonlight stroll past Greystone Church, nestled in England's lush green Cheshire hills. Earlier there had been a wind storm, bringing down a heavy tree limb which flattened a section of the tall iron fence which surrounded the cemetery.

"Let's squeeze through and walk in the graveyard," Fred said.

"What about ghosts?" Annie asked nervously, flicking back her long, auburn hair, then linking her arm in his.

"No such thing," Fred laughed, "and if there were, I'd protect you," he promised. He stepped over the fallen fence, reached for her hand, and helped her wade through the deep sea of ferns. Annie drew up the hem of her pink, ankle length cotton dress and stepped through.

Fred's gray-green, long-sleeved linen shirt, and brown, corduroy pants were still dusted white from the flourmill where he worked. He was tall and broad shouldered, with dark wavy hair and hazel brown eyes. He was more rugged than handsome, Annie decided. They'd met only a week earlier, though it seemed longer. She felt safe with him as they chatted about their simple, uneventful eighteen-year lives.

After walking quietly for a while, they paused briefly for their first awkward kiss, and then sat on a wooden park bench. They held hands in the dark, eerie silence just a few yards away from the tall, heavy wooden gates which guarded the churchyard.

High in the village clock tower, a barn owl hooted, then remained silent until the clock chimed twelve. The full moon drifted in and out of the clouds, casting long shadows among the leaning gravestones, tall crosses and towering granite monuments. Some were two hundred years old, their inscriptions illegible, eroded by weather and time.

Half a dozen bats skimmed silently back and forth, swooping and diving above them. Annie shuddered, pulling tighter on her friend's arm. She was shy but his kiss had been comforting. He'd grown bolder but she had stopped him, preferring that they just talk. Probably hurt, he'd pulled slightly away, lit a cigarette then drew in the smoke.

Earlier that night, a soldier had returned home to their nearby village from the horrors of trench warfare in France. In that year of 1918, Bert Smith won a promotion to sergeant in his Liverpool Scottish Regiment. Tonight he was home for the first time in four years. Home for a brief leave away from the stinking hell of muddy trenches and shell holes. Nine-hundred-thousand British soldiers had fallen and died there. Bert had survived against impossible odds, from the mustard gas and constant shelling. He'd led bayonet charges through minefields, shivered through four, cruel winters. With others, he'd foraged like animals for food among the shelled, jagged remains of French farmhouses. He had dragged dead carcasses of pigs, chickens and geese, back to their trenches for food.

When ordered to attack, he'd scrambled over sandbags, crawled through snaking barbed wire fences, then charged forward into the withering German machine gun fire during the Battle of the River Somme. Sixty thousand British soldiers had fallen and died on that single day.

When I was a small boy, that soldier, *Albert Smith, my granddad,* described how a lone bagpiper had kept playing, still standing, though wounded himself. He played on, throughout the shelling, the gas, explosions and slaughter as hundreds stumbled and fell, before dying in the mud. That piper won the Victoria Cross, Britain's highest award for bravery.

Granddad survived the war with just a wound from a spent bullet in his thigh. He lay for six weeks in an army hospital recovering from his wound and racked with dysentery. Granddad rarely spoke of those horrors.

Sixty years after that war, while in his late eighties, I visited my grandfather. He had ignored my persistent loud knocking on his front door. Finally I climbed through his kitchen window. There he stood, straight-backed, to attention. Alone there, in the darkness of his living room, lit only by the flickering coal-fire. His eyes were open wide, staring ahead, though he no longer could see. The slow forming, snow-white cataracts having made him completely blind.

"Are you alright, granddad?" I asked.

"Yes, I'm sorry son. I heard your knocking," he said. "but I couldn't leave my post."

On reaching his home in the village two hours earlier, Albert Smith's father welcomed him before breaking the awful news. Albert's mother had died three months earlier with pneumonia. She'd written often, but the letters had stopped. Never having learned of her death, he'd brought his mom flowers.

The youngest of thirteen children, Albert was always in trouble. 'Hungry for attention,' folk said. He's 'mom's favorite,' his siblings had whispered, *and he knew that it was true.* On this first night home, late though it was he was now determined to place flowers on his mom's grave.

The massive, seven-foot-high, heavy wooden gates towered above him and were locked tight. Greystone Church cemetery was closed. Two, great, sandstone pillars stood sentry- like, supporting those massive gates. Huge iron hinges spanned the thick, horizontal beams. The thick iron studs held the timbers together as on a medieval castle. A high, spiked iron fence enclosed the entire churchyard. Impenetrable though it seemed, there was nothing which would stop him from visiting his mother's grave that night. For minutes he studied the forbidding gates. He still wore his uniform because he wanted his mom to share in his pride. To see him dressed in his khaki tunic, his Glengarry cap, Scottish kilt, sporran trimmed with horsehair, his Skean Dhu dirk, the emerald-studded dagger tucked into one sock.

Albert thought back to his early army days. Back to the very beginning when they all were so innocent, little more than boys.

They'd marched proudly to their ship, their kilts swinging, the bagpipes playing, the crowds waving and cheering. Pretty young women lined the streets pressing flowers into their hands and throwing them kisses. As the young soldiers sang, marching onward like lambs to the slaughter.

Tonight he would talk to his mom. He knew that she would see him as she looked down from heaven. She'd watch him in his uniform, kneeling and praying by her grave in the moonlight.

Albert tucked his bouquet of flowers into his tunic and began his climb. Freddie had now finished his smoke. Annie watched as the bats circled silently against the moonlit sky. Nearby the tall, black, jagged trees groaned in the breeze, their branches waving as if reaching down for her. She shuddered in the empty silence of the damp, cold night air.

A scraping, grunting sound and sudden movement above the cemetery gates caught Annie's attention. She stiffened, screamed, and jumped to her feet. Freddie turned and glanced upward at the black, writhing, shapeless, figure with its arms outstretched as it leapt into space. Twenty feet away, the thing landed heavily onto the gravel path, before flapping and rolling into the shadows.

Freddie too was now on his feet, yelling and running faster than he'd ever run. He raced down the path towards the opening in the fallen fence, his arms flailing, his heart pounding. Bushes and trees blurred past him in the darkness. Annie was already gone. Fred heard her screaming as she ran away in the opposite direction. The creature was probably close behind her.

'What was it?' he asked himself while running, never once stopping until he was safely home.

He fumbled for his door key, crept up to his bed, and lay down fully dressed. He wondered about Annie and felt deeply ashamed, hoping that she was safe. It was too late for him to do anything. This was only their second date after meeting in the local pub a week earlier. He didn't know where she lived. He knew he'd acted cowardly, but hell, what was that thing? A vampire? What else would be flying around a graveyard wearing a cape at midnight?

Three nights later he saw Annie again in the Unicorn Arms. She stood whispering with two girlfriends at the bar. She glanced his way, he smiled and waved, but she ignored him. He moved over to her.

"I'm sorry," he said. She didn't answer, just glanced away.

"Please forgive me Annie. I panicked. That bloody thing scared the hell out of me," he whispered, not wanting her friends to hear.

"Me too," she said coldly, before turning away for the final time. He knew that it was over. Nothing more was said between them, not then, not ever. Cowardice was something which no-one could tolerate. Not now, not after thousands of brave men had died and the wounded were still dying.

Neither Annie nor Fred realized that they'd be forever linked by their night together in that graveyard. That each, on countless occasions throughout their lives would describe their terrifying experience to all who'd listen. Each was convinced they had brushed with death on that awful night. With each telling, their story grew. All who heard it agreed that it was best to stay clear of Greystone Churchyard at night. The local folk had many explanations. Some said it was a witch, others a werewolf. Most believed that a vampire was on the prowl that night.

It was many years later before my Granddad heard the story. A week after that strange night, he was shipped, along with his Liverpool Scottish Regiment to Ireland, to deal with, *'The Troubles.'*

During the year that he was away, the legend of the Greystone Vampire was born, and quickly spread. It remains alive to this very day, whispered along with the mysteries and folklore of England's verdant, gently rolling Cheshire hills.

NATIVE AMERICAN

A RNOLD WAS TALL, RED-HAIRED, SLIM *and very English.* In 1962, the week before Thanksgiving, he began working as a draftsman in upstate New York.

He and his wife Mary were twenty-four and recently married. Eight weeks earlier they had emigrated from England. They found that many things were different from life in the UK. There were subtle, cultural, and many unexpected differences.

Arnold had the unfortunate knack of saying the wrong thing without ever intending to. He frequently offended people. This was mainly because many common British words have a different meaning to Americans.

Arnold didn't know this. In England he was known for being polite and caring. He was never the sort of bloke who'd intentionally hurt anyone's feelings. But here, Arnold seemed to be forever stumbling and insulting people.

The first instance was while visiting and drinking coffee in his neighbor Fred's, kitchen. Fred's seventeen year-old-daughter was overweight, and her hair was in rollers. She was busy baking brownies. Arnold, in his effort to make polite conversation, told Fred that his daughter was very homely. Naturally his neighbor Fred was hurt. Arnold, believing that Fred had somehow misunderstood him, he repeated, "Your daughter's very homely, isn't she?"

"I heard you the first time," his neighbor snapped, before showing Arnold to the door and bidding him goodbye. Later, Fred learned that 'homely,' didn't mean 'home loving' or, 'handy in the kitchen,' as it did in England.

On his first day in the engineering drawing office of the company, he was introduced to his fellow employees.

Graham Wolf was both engineer and Native American. His desk was beside Arnold's drawing board. "I should warn you about him," Frank, his boss said.

"He prefers the name Gray Wolf and is very proud of his Indian heritage. He was born on a Canadian reservation where living conditions were pretty rough. Gray Wolf is real sensitive and bitter about the way his native people were treated throughout history by us whites. He gets real mad when anyone pokes fun at his people," Frank explained.

"We try not to upset him because he'll brood for days."

"I can well understand that. I'd never dream of saying anything hurtful," Arnold said, and meant it.

As Arnold and Frank approached, Gray Wolf pushed back his chair and stood. He was tall and straight-backed, with jet black, shoulder length hair. He had strong, rugged features and was unsmiling. He stared for a moment at Arnold's outstretched hand before taking it. During Gray Wolf's introduction he didn't speak, only nodded. Arnold felt his piercing dark eyes, reading him with suspicion.

A half hour later, the Englishman had met all those he'd work with. Most were his senior. He remarked casually, "Obviously I'm the low man on the totem pole."

"Totem pole!" Gray Wolf repeated, while glaring angrily at Arnold.

"Oops, sorry," Arnold said weakly, as everyone stared.

Later, on recognizing the high number of supervisors in the company, he offered casually,

"Looks like there're more chiefs than Indians."

"Excuse me?" Gray Wolf snapped, giving him a look which he'd never forget.

"Sorry. Just an expression," he added weakly. "Keep your hair on. Oops . . . I didn't mean that," he said, embarrassed by his clumsiness.

Though Arnold had a variety of pencils and drawing instruments, he sometimes needed drafting tape, and paper clips.

"See Margie for any stationery supplies," the guys told him. While making a change to an engineering drawing he asked a fellow draftsman for a rubber.

"Ask Margie," they said, then watching as he walked over to her desk.

"May I have a rubber?" he asked politely. Margie gasped, and then blushed beet red.

"Why are you asking me?" she stammered.

"'Cause they told me you keep the supplies," Arnold explained, gesturing toward the guys, who by now were doubled over with laughter.

"I do, *but not those,*" she said, her face still red.

"Well I need to change my drawing and have to rub out some pencil lines."

"Oh. You need *an eraser,*" she said, glaring at the laughing guys as she opened her cabinet.

Each lunch-time Gray Wolf ate at his desk while reading his newspaper. He'd also answer the boss's phone. As the manager left the office for the company cafeteria,

"Watch the fort," he said while passing Gray Wolf's desk.

Arnold glanced up, and chuckled. "You find that funny?" Gray Wolf snapped. "Frank asking an Indian to watch the fort? The fox guarding the chickens . . ."

"No! I've never heard that expression before. It's funny because, in England my boss would say, 'I'm off for a bit of lunch. Answer my phone, old chap?'

"Gray Wolf gave a slight smile, accepting his explanation."

In the passing weeks Arnold made fewer goofs and Gray Wolf relaxed around him. He now viewed him less as a threat and more of a dumb, thoughtless foreigner.

Arnold liked Gray Wolf. He saw him as a quiet, hard working, nice guy. In an effort to become friends, he asked Gray Wolf and his girl friend to join he and his wife for dinner. They chose a classy, though pricey restaurant in a good section of the city. They arranged to meet in the parking lot. Arnold's wife was looking forward to meeting Gray Wolf. She'd heard so much about him.

It promised to be a wonderful evening. And well it may have been. If not for that awful moment when at the restaurant's entrance, when the Maître 'D greeted them with,

"Good evening folks. ***Do you have a reservation?***"

TOUGH JOB

WHEN GREG AND HIS WIFE Jenny bought *The Beehive,* Greg at last realized his lifetime's ambition of owning a pub. Chuck and his wife Maggie, their two best friends, thought Greg was nuts. They tried talking him out of it, but failed. Call it mid-life crisis, ambition, whatever, but, 'Greg the dreamer,' wouldn't listen.

Neither Greg nor Jenny had a clue on how to run a business. They'd enjoyed many hours on the fun side of bars, so they figured, 'how hard could it be?' They certainly knew their way around booze, hamburgers, and chili.

Owning a pub is most guys' dream. Greg needed to get away from his current job and his loser boss, who didn't know his ass from a hole in the ground. Greg pictured himself joking and serving drinks to thirsty friends and customers. Then, later that night he and Jenny could enjoy counting wads of money.

Greg was short, stocky, and energetic. The guy who'd never quit. Jenny was heavy, nervous and a hopeless worrywart. When things got tough, she'd quit, make a pitcher of Manhattan, and then while sitting amid the chaos, relax.

The Beehive's location was great, just a short drive from a college. It had a large parking lot on a busy road leading to New York's Adirondack Mountains. The downside was that the place needed major repairs. A section of gutter was missing causing water damage to a lower wall. Two broken windows were covered with a plastic. The parking lot was dotted with cracks and crumbling patches.

The previous owners were old and in poor health. It had been closed for a year and the pub's interior was dirty and shabby. But the plumbing, electrical, and heating systems were sound and the kitchen equipment was in good shape. Greg, Jenny and their two close friends spent their vacation cleaning and painting the inside. When they'd finished, the pub looked great.

Greg and Jenny were in their late forties. This venture had drained their lifesavings, leaving them spread thin, financially. Closing costs, insurance, and liquor license fees were much higher than they expected. Their two, teenage daughters, upset at leaving their friends, were of little help.

Though Chuck had little experience, he offered to help bartending. He figured that Greg would never take him up on his offer, but he did, proving he was desperate.

Ernie the regular bartender came with the place. He'd been both resident and bartender for over four years. He was divorced, in his late thirties and lived above the Bee Hive in a messy, one bed- room apartment. Greg and Chuck re-painted Ernie's bathroom, washed his drapes, and shampooed his carpet. But Ernie insisted that his apartment remain in its current, chaotic state of extreme clutter. Greg honored Ernie's wishes mostly because he needed him.

Chuck never asked Greg if Ernie lived there rent-free, or what their deal was. Ernie simply drifted along, fixing himself a sandwich, pouring a drink, and feeding coins into the cigarette machine. This arrangement, which to Chuck seemed odd, evidently suited Greg. Jenny ran the kitchen, Greg the business and family issues, and Ernie took care of the bar.

The wall behind the bar was painted with black and yellow, bee-like, vertical stripes. On that same wall was a large mirror below which were glass shelves of assorted liquor bottles. Four, hand sized, plastic bees hung on fishing line from the ceiling. They twirled slowly around in the ever present cigarette smoke.

To the left of the bar, were the rest rooms, marked 'Drones' and 'Queens. If a guy staggered through the wrong door, a chorus of jeers erupted from the bar crowd. The Bee Hives customers were mostly blue collar. Draft and bottled beer was the norm. When hungry, they ordered a cheeseburger or a bowl of Jenny's chili. Down the hall by the kitchen, was a small restaurant section. There were few customers when they first opened but Greg and Jenny planned on changing that.

Ernie the bartender was tall, slim, good-looking, likable, and quick to smile. A cigarette seemed glued to his lips and he was rarely sober. He had dark hair, sleepy brown eyes and his shoulders were stooped as if laden with problems. His crumpled shirt, torn jeans, and dirty sneakers, gave him a sad, lost look. He lived alone, but rarely lacked female company.

When Ernie learned of Chuck's offer to work on Friday evenings and most of Saturday, he was thrilled. On that first Saturday morning, Ernie welcomed Chuck with an enthusiastic bear hug.

Ernie's hair was unkempt and he smelled of smoke and booze. He looked haggard, his eyes bloodshot, and his face puffy.

"Hey Chuck, great to see you," he rasped.

"Last night was a friggin' zoo. At one time we had two fights raging and Greg had to call the cops. I didn't hit the sack 'til dawn," Ernie said, his cigarette bouncing on his lip and the beer bottle in his hand, shaking. After giving Chuck a quick bartending course and a list of prices, Ernie sighed as though suddenly free.

"You'll do fine," he told Chuck.

"It's mostly a beer joint. For fancy drinks, my Bartender's Guide Book's under the bar."

Half an hour later, Chuck was alone but warmed quickly to the job. While moving along the bar he caught bits of odd conversation.

"They released me from the County Jail last week," one whispered.

"You'd never believe the crap that goes on there. Night-time's the worst 'cause in the dark, your mind plays tricks. Some nights you hear guys crying' and moaning' and you wonder if they're bein' raped or comin' down off drugs. One guy hung himself with strips from his blanket."

Chuck took a liking to Sam, a retired old trucker.

"Tomorrow's my eighty-third birthday," Sam said, sucking deeply on his cigarette before exhaling the smoke through his nose.

"My birthday's good for free beer, right?" he said, looking straight at Chuck.

"Better check with Greg," Chuck said, grinning.

For an old guy, Sam's gray eyes were bright, and his humor quick and funny. He worked at staying young and kept up with world news. He wore a red flannel shirt, jeans, sneakers and a Yankee baseball cap.

"I come here for a break away from girlfriends," Sam bragged. "Give 'em half a chance, and they'll run your life."

"Did you say *girlfriends*?" Chuck asked.

"Yeah, I've got two of 'em. Both are in their mid-sixties. I always preferred older women, but at my age there's not many still around," Sam said, as laughter rippled along the bar.

"They're both good lookin' and built nice. 'Course neither one's perfect. If I could find all their good qualities in one woman, I'd marry her."

"Which qualities are those?" Chuck asked.

"Well, one's a great cook, owns her home and treats me like a king," Sam said.

"The other's a lousy cook and housekeeper, dirt poor, but dynamite in the sack." "Yeah, that's a tough choice," Chuck offered before moving up the bar.

At noon, Ernie stopped by to re-fill the beer cooler.

"I'm exhausted, and need to hit the sack," he said. "If anyone's looking for me, tell 'em I'm out shopping."

"Will do," Chuck said, watching as he headed for the stairs.

Chuck wiped the bar top, washed a few glasses, filled the potato-chip rack, and then pumped two draft beers.

A half hour later, a striking blonde in a pale pink dress walked in and slid onto a bar stool She rested a white linen-covered pie dish on the bar, then beckoned to Chuck with a red-nailed manicured finger. As he moved closer, she touched the finger tip to her lips, signaling secrecy.

"Is Ernie upstairs?" she purred.

"No, he's grocery shopping," Chuck said.

"Yeah, right," she whispered. "When did he buy groceries? Good try though. He loves my apple pie," she giggled, before scooping up her dish and wiggling up the stairs. An hour later she waved to Chuck before leaving.

The bar grew busier, noisier and filled with cigarette smoke. The jukebox bounced with a mixture of country and rock music. Fifty minutes after Ernie's earlier visitor had left, a second lady stopped by the bar.

"I need change for cigarettes," she said.

She was attractive, in her mid-thirties, with short black hair. She wore a dark blue, tailored pants suit which suggested she may have just left a corporate office meeting.

Chuck dropped the change in her hand and noticed an engagement ring and wedding band along with a whiff of expensive perfume.

"Is he upstairs?" she asked, her voice low and husky.

"No, Ernie's out," Chuck said.

"Then I'll wait in his apartment. He's loaning me a book," she explained, before feeding money into the cigarette machine and heading upstairs.

Chuck felt bad. He should have fought harder for Ernie's rest, his health and well-being. The guy was physically and emotionally weak. Powerless against the cruel, selfish demands which these ladies were making on him.

Two hours later Chuck watched as the lady crept out through the exit. He saw no sign of the book which she needed.

At six that evening, Ernie stopped by the bar. Though his face was pale, haggard and drawn, his hair was combed. He had showered, shaved and smelled of cologne. He wore a sharp looking, navy blue blazer, neatly pressed tan slacks, and brown loafers. He looked as though heading for church. Chuck marveled at the change in Ernie's appearance.

"Pour me a double Red Label scotch with just a splash," Ernie said. "And put it on my tab,"

"What tab? Give me a break," Chuck said, grinning while pouring the drink.

"I need it to take off the edge." Ernie said. "This is my first night out in weeks."

"Why are you going out?" Chuck asked. "Everythin' you could need's right here, even home delivery," Chuck said, while laughing.

"You think my life's funny?" Ernie said, his voice dry.

"Well, it's not. This bar, the smoke, booze and endless women are killing me. Your life has purpose . . . some meaning. You're an engineer, right? There's satisfaction in that. What do I have to show for mine? I'm old at thirty-three. Women take advantage. They use me. I'm just a plaything. My life's a living hell," he said, before lighting a cigarette, downing his drink, then weaving out into the fading light.

Ernie's words, 'living hell,' have haunted Chuck ever since.

He wondered, 'given the chance, how many guys would swap their lives for Ernie's?'

Chuck compared his typical day, with Ernie's.

Chuck's day began at five-thirty, followed by an hour long drive in angry, honking, crawling traffic. Then, began his stressful, thankless job, of incessant ringing phones, while designing an endless stream of printed circuit boards. His boss hated him, and set impossible production targets. The threat of losing his job was the penalty of failure. Chuck thought of his bills, his three children who no longer spoke to him, his wife's anger toward him, and he questioned his life.

In stark contrast, there was Ernie's typical day. Each morning he awoke, made toast, fixed himself a drink, borrowed change from the cash drawer for smokes, and then awaited the visiting ladies.

Though Ernie's life was empty, with free booze, endless sex and no responsibility, it had a certain appeal.

Of course, no intelligent, mature, responsible guy one would ever seriously consider trading their life with Ernie's . . . *would they?*

NOTHING STOPS KOWALSKI

JAKUB KOWALSKI WAS BORN IN Poland in 1945, just as the Second World War was ending. Poland's cities lay in charred, crumbling ruins. Its economy, manufacturing, and its food supply were virtually non-existent. Jakub's family was poor and many years of hardship lay ahead.

When Jakub was ten, tall for his age, skinny, and athletic, he had bright blue eyes and an unruly mop of thick, blonde hair. The youngest of eleven children, he lived and worked on their small farm in Kazakski in southeastern Poland. His brothers and sisters helped with chores from the time they could walk. Each morning, Jakub arose early to feed their chickens and gather eggs. Later, he shoveled manure before dumping it beside the woods. When rotted, he spread it onto their vegetable garden, for little was ever wasted. Jakub kept rabbits in a wire run, which every few days he'd drag farther along the meadow. His rabbits ate a plentiful supply of fresh clover, alfalfa, and hay. He never named his rabbits because they were not pets. They were raised for meat, and their fur became gloves or the warm linings for boots and winter jackets.

Their cows gave them milk, butter and cheese. When a cow gave birth, the female calves were raised for milking and the bullocks were sold at the town market. Sickly cows, unfit to sell, were slaughtered for meat. Chickens were prized and roamed freely. They produced fresh eggs and ate the bugs in their vegetable garden. Surplus chickens and eggs were sold at market. The chicken's droppings were added to the manure pile. Jakub dug the earthworms from his manure to sell to fisherman as they walked to the river. The money bought his schoolbooks. When the weather was fair, Jakub would also fish. When fish were very plentiful Jakub's grandma Babka, would cook, or preserve them. She'd clean, then either cure them in the smokehouse or pack them in salt, preserving them in a wooden cask in the cellar. Grandma Babka was short, heavy, and red-faced. She wore a colorful, silk headscarf over her pure white hair. On cold days, she wore a gray knitted shawl over her dark blue dress.

They grew apples and pears which were eaten fresh, or stored in the root cellar. Fallen apples were gathered, and then made into cider, or vinegar. Pears, plums, blackberries and cherries, made jam, and sometimes wine, which the adults drank on birthdays and at Christmas. Grandma Babka kept bees. Her honey was for cooking, baking, and making toffee. She alone cared for the bees, as most folk were afraid of them. Her grandchildren believed the bees would never dare sting grandma. *Probably because of the big wooden spoon which hung from her apron. No bee would risk a whack with that thing.* Grandma Babka made pickles, preserved fruit and vegetables in jars which she sealed tight with beeswax. She also made 'juice' from her honey and wine. Jakub loved watching the older family members sing and dance after drinking 'grandma's juice.'

Jakub's family drank their fresh cow's milk. The left over cream was churned into butter and cheese. Grandma Babka also kept pigs and geese.

'She uses every part of her hogs, except their squeal,' folk joked. The meat was mostly smoked to make bacon, ham and pork chops. Grandma loved her pigs. Everyone said that she loved those greedy, squabbling, mean tempered animals more than her family. When a sow was close to having babies, grandma read her stories. Jakub would listen wide-eyed, while cuddled in a sheepskin blanket. The flickering oil lamp, threw dancing shadows as the wind whistled through the barn's siding. Cows chomped contentedly, as their stomachs rumbled. Jakub loved those times. His grandma was a wonderful storyteller. The earthy, barn-smell of the fresh hay and farm animals, was comforting to Jakub. This was home, and all that he knew.

Grandma Babka enriched her stories by using different voices and funny sounds. Often she'd make him laugh. But sometimes she told sad stories which made him cry. It was okay for him to cry when he was with his grandma. But he could never cry when with his father, or older brothers. *Polish boys and men were not permitted to cry.* Tears were for babies, girls, or mothers who'd lost her child.

Often when pigs give birth, one baby is sickly and weak. Without help it would die. The bigger, more aggressive piglets bullied and jostled it, leaving it little chance of finding a nipple. Jakub's grandma once gave him a weak little pig for his own. He named it Peppy, because it was a feisty, spirited little thing. Jakub pushed away the stronger piglets so that Peppy could share his mother's milk. When his piglet was big and healthy, Jakub sold him at the market. He'd learned early the importance of never giving up, of keeping on, regardless of the circumstances. He knew that with persistence, eventually you will win. Jakub's brothers were older, bigger, and stronger. He related with those weak little pigs. He learned that all life was precious. It was also a valuable business lesson.

"Never quit," his grandma would lecture. But Jakub already knew that. He never gave up, no matter what.

"That boy has a will of steel," his grandma said of him. "He will go far." Her words had great influence on Jakub. He listened, remembered, and took them to heart.

Because Jakub was skinny, the bigger boys bullied him. They teased him because his clothes were patched, the hand-me-downs from his older brothers. When knocked down, Jakub fought back, he scrambled back up, and went right back at his opponent. When his nose bled he wiped it on his shirt sleeve and kept going, with both fists flying. Finally, when both lay exhausted in the mud, the fight ended in a draw. On realizing that this scrappy kid would never quit, the bullying ended.

His grandfather once noticed bruises on Jakub's face and his fat lip. He taught him to box and Jakub won his next fight with a much bigger opponent. His teachers watched, shook their heads, and smiled.

"Jakub's too big for our small village," they whispered together. He wouldn't fight again until he was a grown man. When fifteen he left school. He was taller and his shoulders broader. His arms were muscular and his hands big and strong from shoveling, baling hay, and carrying countless pails of milk.

He'd killed chickens when he was nine. Later, a pig, and finally their old cow when he was fourteen. That had been the hardest for Jakub had milked that cow many times and helped it deliver four baby calves. When it was too old to give milk and have calves, his father told him to kill it. Jakub had walked it four times around the oak tree until its head was tethered hard against the trunk. Then, he'd slit its throat, catching the spurting blood in his bucket to make sausage. He'd hated killing it, but knew that it wasn't a cruel thing. For death was part of farm life. Some things die so that others may live. He hadn't written that law, he merely lived by it. He never killed for sport as others did. He killed, only for food. When he was older, he'd kill for other reasons. But that was much later, at a different time, in another life.

When Jakub was ten he witnessed the death of his grandfather. His granddad had been careless and turned his back on their old, ill-tempered, big black bull. The animal had first gored, driven, and then crushed him against the barn. He next tossed his granddad's lifeless body like a heavy old sack into the weeds. Jakub loved his fine, hard-working, old granddad. He'd wanted to kill that bull, but was too young. Aleksy, his seventeen-year-old brother had done it for him.

They'd butchered the bull, and then salted its meat for storing in a barrel. After stripping the fur from its hide, they tanned it with oak bark, stretched it on wooden frames, and dried it in the sun. From the leather, their father made boots and scabbards for hunting knives and for Jakub's axe which he used to chop wood for winter.

"You have woodcutter's hands," his father told him. It was true. Jakub's hands were big and powerful. They'd chopped down many trees, hewed, and then sawed them into planks. With a mule he'd pulled huge stubborn tree stumps.

As Jakub drew closer to manhood, he hungered for whatever lay beyond the distant, green, mist-cloaked, towering hills which sheltered their farm from the fierce northern winds.

On his eighteenth birthday, he packed a few clothes, some cheese, smoked fish, sausage, and two loaves into his rabbit-skin backpack. After kissing his family goodbye, he set out, striding up the familiar, long dusty road. As he rounded the tree-lined bend, he waved one last time. He couldn't help his eyes filling with tears. He knew that he may never see his family again. The road ahead stretched for four hundred miles to Gdynia, a large port on the Baltic Sea. He'd work odd jobs at farms along the way usually for just a day, sometimes two, but always he headed north.

One night he stopped at a gypsy camp. He was hungry, they had a fire, and he needed company. Anna was a gypsy woman in her late seventies. Her smile was twisted, *perhaps by a stroke,* Jakub wondered. She walked stooped over, leaning on her gnarled, hickory cane.

"She sees your fortune in your palms," they whispered. 'Maybe the horrors of what she sees in folk's hands, weighs on her shoulders?' he wondered.

Jakub sat on a fallen log and stared into the fire. He was tormented by the smell from the bubbling black iron pot which hung above it. Anna hobbled over, bent down slowly, and sat beside him. A brightly colored, paisley shawl draped her head and shoulders. Her brown, coarse woolen dress was darned and patched. Her face and hands reminded Jakub of weathered, tired old leather.

"For two zloty I read your fortune and maybe bring you luck, "Anna said, her voice low, and raspy.

"With so little money I must make my own luck," Jakub said.

"My grandfather warned me that all fortune tellers are fakes."

Anna glanced quickly up from the flames, and smiled. Her teeth were broken and stained. "Not all are fakes," she said. "It is sad I never met your grandfather. I would have warned him of his black bull."

Jakub stiffened. *How could she have known of the bull?* He stared at her for a long, long time. After sharing the rabbit stew, he sat with

Anna beneath an old pine tree. She leaned closer to him, studying his open palms by the light of a whale-oil lamp. "These are farmer's hands," she said, her voice just a whisper. "Your life it now changes. You visit new lands and sail over great seas. Pain and death follows closely in your footsteps. One day the dark angel, he catches you. Then, your heart it breaks and your hands fill with your tears," she said, sighing deeply, while watching his eyes.

"Enough rubbish!" Jakub said, standing suddenly, refusing to hear more.

"Are these the hands of a man who cries?" he asked angrily, holding them up to her face. "Tears are for women and children. A man must be stronger than that." He tossed two coins into her lap before striding quickly away into the darkness.

"I'm sorry," she said, calling after him, "I tell you only what I see. I have no power to stop the tears caused by your great pain." Having heard enough, he crawled into his bedroll beneath a weeping willow. Though tired, he lay awake for a while. The old woman's words troubled him. Weakness was a shameful thing. She had been right about the bull. But there was nothing which would make Jakub cry.

A crowing rooster from a nearby farm awakened him. He bought eggs and milk, and then bathed in a mountain stream. On good days he'd walk twenty-five miles. Sometimes, he rode with farmers on horse-drawn carts and learned news of work. He heard distant trains but he couldn't pay. He thought of climbing aboard slow moving freights, but daren't risk trouble. There were many desperate, hungry men who robbed and killed. It was better to avoid such people. From Gdynia, he'd find work on ships bound for Canada, or America. In churches he'd buy candles and pray. Magda, his teacher, had taught him a little English. She lived in America for two years and had a world map on their classroom wall. Jakub memorized the names of seaports and big cities where he might find work.

He hired onto a ship bound for Montreal, Canada. The pay and food was poor and he was seasick. The crew laughed as he hung over the side, but soon he was back at work again. "Nothing stops

Kowalski," they said amid their laughter. From Montreal he caught a freighter to New York City.

In 1964, the war was growing in Vietnam. With help, he applied for his green card and took a physical examination. He learned it would take weeks to process, so he hired onto a ship bound for South America.

With his green card approved, he registered for the military draft, and took another physical. Five months later, he was drafted into the U.S. Army. He liked basic training, found the food good, and enjoyed a hot shower each day. They gave him a uniform and boots, the first new clothes he'd ever owned. They even paid him and he liked the vigorous training. His fellow soldiers teased him for his poor English and called him dumb Polack. He didn't mind. In fact enjoyed the good-natured kidding of the guys he bunked with. He was proud of being Polish, but becoming American offered a better life. One where he may one day own a house and raise a family. To have these things, he knew that first he must prove himself worthy.

Soon after basic training, he learned his outfit was being shipped to Vietnam. He'd heard of that country but didn't know where it was. They told him that Vietcong soldiers were killing Americans. That was why they had trained him to fight them. Two months after arriving in Nam, they made him squad leader. They saw that he had 'the right stuff.' "Nothing stops Kowalski," men said of him. After many patrols through Vietnam's jungles they called him a hard-nosed Polack because, 'he took no crap.' He was tough, insisting his men moved silently through that stinking, crawling heat, and mosquito infested swamps and oozing, endless rice paddies. All radio transmission was minimal, with no beer, pot, cigarettes, or even gum. When on patrols, no one talked. They used only hand signals. "Hell, we ain't allowed to fart," they said. On their first patrol, he ordered his men to sit, wait, and listen in total silence. Jakub then led a young soldier a mile farther ahead along the jungle trail. He then sat with him on a fallen tree, where they talked quietly for twenty minutes. On their return, his squad was oddly quiet. They were amazed how

Jakub's and the rookie's voices had carried. They never forgot the lesson which probably saved lives. Jakub led them from the front, never asking anyone to do anything he wouldn't. Never once were they ambushed. Instead it was <u>they</u> who caught their enemy off guard.

Jakub's men moved as shadows. For days, they would lie in silence, reading, writing home, or in their journals. Their watchwords were, 'silent and still.' Above them, high in the trees, the birds and monkeys called and chattered together. As the Victcong approached, the creatures grew silent. The VC believed it was their presence which brought the silence. By then it was too late for them. Jakub's squad killed many without ever losing a man. His men no longer called him Polack. Now, he was simply Jake. He liked that because, though still a foreigner with a thick accent, he knew they now accepted him.

On nights when in safe territory they smoked and swapped yarns. Soldiers love stories, even those which are untrue. Jake learned of life in the mean streets of America's big cities. Of drug sales gone bad, of drive-by shootings and gang warfare. But no one had stories like Jakub. He described his life on his farm. He repeated his father's stories of the German invasion of Poland. He described the photographs he'd seen of Polish civilians hanging from each telephone pole stretching to the horizon.

When Jakub was a small boy, a rooster spurred his face leaving an ugly scar from his left eye to his upper lip. When his mother sewed the wound closed, he hadn't cried. She'd called him, 'her brave little soldier,' before rewarding him with a slice of apple pie.

During one all-night 'bull session,' he told his squad that his scar resulted from a sword fight with a Cossack over a brown-eyed peasant girl. They'd laughed, called him a lying bastard but never tired of the story.

When his army life ended, he found work at a furniture factory in South Carolina. The hours were long, but the overtime helped buy a five-year-old truck. He joined Polska Kola, a Polish social club where he met a Polish girl, named Lidia. Though her parents came from Poland, Lidia was born in the USA. She spoke Polish well, and

Jakub enjoyed speaking in his native tongue again. Lidia helped him improve his English.

Six months after they met, they married and bought a small raised ranch with a two-car garage. Their blacktop driveway lay four feet below their front lawn. A large, dense, forsythia bush hid the steep, granite path leading down to their driveway.

A year after buying their home, they were blessed with a baby boy. They named him Dawid. His hair was blonde, and his bright blue eyes and smile would light up a room. Dawid was three when Santa Claus brought him his bright red tricycle. He never tired of ringing his shiny chrome bell as he pedaled up and down their blacktop driveway.

Since early childhood Jakub had been a risk taker. His life had made him that way. It was his script. 'No one can wait until everything's perfect. You must make do with what you have. Play the cards you're dealt. Keep going no matter what. Never let obstacles block you. Life's a gamble . . . with no guarantees.' Jakub had always believed in making his own luck.

One beautiful crisp morning in early fall, as Jakub headed down his front path for work, he noticed a small pool of oil beneath his truck. Fluid dripped slowly from the brake line. He could phone into work claiming to be sick. But this wasn't a good time. Four weeks earlier, they learned another baby was due in the coming year. Work was slow because of the increased imports from China. Jakub hadn't worked overtime for a year and there were rumors of layoffs. He phoned his mechanic to have the leaking brake line fixed the next day. It was risky driving with bad brakes but Jakub's truck had standard shift. He'd slow down by downshifting gears. He topped up his brake fluid, but on his drive home, his brakes grew worse.

He was only doing 6 mph as he swung into his driveway. A blur of blue flashed down the steep path in front of him. It was Dawid, in his sailor suit, riding his tricycle, wildly ringing his bell, excited to see his daddy. Dawid hurtled down the steep path in front of him. Jakub glimpsed his blonde, three year-old son disappear beneath the front of his truck. Jakub's brake pedal slammed hard to the floor. A squealing, metallic grinding, screech was followed by a child's short cry, a split second before Jakub's front wheels jumped, and his truck smashed into his garage door.

Jakub killed his engine, jumped out of his cab, knelt, and crawled between his truck's front wheels. He reached helplessly into the mangled tricycle frame of limbs, head and flesh. The tattered remnants of his little boy's sailor suit and Jakub's forearms lay in a growing pool of warm oil, radiator fluid, and blood. A low, guttural, barely human moaning sound became a terrible howling. It came up from somewhere deep within Jakub's chest and increased into a long, uncontrollable, agonizing scream.

Much later, with head bowed, his face buried in the palm of both hands, Jakub began to cry. No one could reach him. Not even his wife already heavily sedated and staying with her parent's.

For six days and nights Jakub didn't sleep. He screamed continually as if in agony, thrashing as if living a nightmare. He neither ate nor drank, until, completely exhausted he fell asleep. Even while unconscious, he cried and sobbed bitterly. After twelve hours, Jakub no longer had tears, only heavy breathing.

Kowalski had finally stopped.

ORCHIDS

*T*HE *GALLEY* WAS MCTAVISH'S LOCAL pub. Each evening after work he'd leave *Flash,* his Greyhound, tied to his bike outside while he enjoyed a few pints of beer. His tweed cap, black boots, grey shirt and overalls were usually stained with plaster and paint from his contractor work. Though still in his late twenties, he had little enthusiasm for hard work.

This was Scotland in 1946. The nightmare of World War Two was over. A mixture of displaced people sailed in and out of Glasgow, Scotland's largest seaport. *The Galley* was a magnet, drawing travelers from every corner of the world. They came for a pint, a game of darts, a few laughs, and a brief escape.

One typical Saturday night McTavish met the sailor from Guatemala. At first their conversation was awkward. McTavish's Scottish accent was so thick, that even Englishmen could barely understand him. How McTavish and the Guatemalan managed to communicate was baffling. Either chance or fate sat them on adjoining stools at the bar on that July night. McTavish ordered a pint, stuck a cigarette between his lips, and fumbled for a match. The Guatemalan sailor pressed the burning tip of his Cuban cigar to the end of McTavish's cigarette. This simple act changed McTavish's life forever, for as he nodded his thanks, their strange conversation began. Neither understood the other well, but the beer and smoke somehow helped. McTavish offered his hand, Miguel his, both men grinned, while clinking beer mugs. After swapping names, Miguel pulled an egg-sized, chamois leather pouch from around his neck where it had dangled beside his gold crucifix. He drew open the drawstring and shook out five, small, plump, ivory colored seeds onto the bar.

"Zese leetle seeds soon make me reech. Zay is orchid seeds from Brazil rain forest," he said.

"How's that?" McTavish asked, staring in disbelief.

"What you call 'im . . . flower profezzor man? . . .

"Biologist?" McTavish offered.

"Yez, zis crazee profezzor man, he live years in jungle like monkey. Zis orchid has no name," he said, pausing to knock the ash from his cigar. A gold front tooth glistened and his twisted, wax moustache bounced as he spoke. A lock of greasy black hair dangled from beneath his red bandana. Though still in his mid-forties, he looked older. His face had the dry. wrinkled texture of a leather wallet.

"Crazee profezzor man he gets drunk. Zen 'e play cards. 'E loze all 'iz money. 'E keeps playin'. Is how I win dese seeds. Now diz London flower man 'e come see me. Wants seeds so bad he pay twenty pounds for each."

McTavish did the math. A hundred pounds for five seeds was a year's pay. Minutes later, as Miguel drained his glass, McTavish pushed a half crown forward, and held up two fingers to Elsie the barmaid. Miguel peppered his story with a mish-mash of Spanish and broken English. McTavish followed most of it, and what he understood, he liked.

Evidently, after living for two years somewhere in the mountains of a Brazilian rain forest, a biologist found a new specimen of orchid. Miguel met the explorer in a bar, and then later he'd won *the only five orchid seeds* in the civilized world. McTavish had read somewhere that rich collectors pay thousands of pounds for such rare orchids. Now some biologist, possibly from London's *Kew Gardens*, had offered Miguel twenty pounds for each seed. Miguel wouldn't have a clue as to what they were really worth. But McTavish was pretty smart. He knew that plants would be worth far more than just seeds. He dropped his trembling hands to his lap to hide his excitement. Those long, plump, ivory colored seeds still lay beside Miguel's leather pouch on the bar. McTavish resisted the urge to touch them. They almost glowed in the dim, half light of the noisy, smoky pub.

After three pints, Miguel's interest had strayed from his orchid seeds. His eyes were now fixed on Elsie, the sexy, bottle blond barmaid. She had once been a real beauty but her life had been tough. She'd since packed on a few extra pounds but still had a shape men drooled over. Miguel's eyes were glued on Elsie's low-cut blouse. Each time she bent forward to rinse glasses; he raised up and craned his neck. Elsie noticed and smiled. McTavish caught their brief exchange. Miguel chomped harder on his cigar, as Elsie's perfume, blonde hair, and full red lips, raised his pulse rate. Twice divorced, and in her mid-fifties, Elsie was recently a widow. A year earlier, her husband while drunk, had fallen off a roof.

As McTavish stared hungrily at those orchid seeds, Miguel's obvious interest in Elsie gave the Scotsman an idea. He needed to move fast. An opportunity like this may never come again.

Elsie had seen McTavish's *Hercules* bicycle a month earlier. It had once been his mother's. His *Rolls Royce* of ladies' bicycles had been stored in his dad's dry cellar for years. Still like new, without a scratch on its glossy black frame, McTavish kept the bike's chrome shining. Its chain and mudguards were snow-white. There were *Sturmey-Archer* gears, a wicker basket mounted on the handlebars and a *Brooks*, wide leather saddle. The rear wheel driven dynamo, powered both the front and rear lights.

The bike was now parked outside with *Flash*, his greyhound, tied to it. Each night, as McTavish pedaled between his home and the pub, his dog trotted along for exercise.

Flash was fast. Maybe the fastest greyhound in Scotland. He'd raced eleven times and won them all. Miguel had heard of *Flash* and wanted him. But until he sold those orchid seeds, he had no money. Miguel sailed in three days for Venezuela and wanted *Flash* to go with him. Apparently dog-racing was very big there. The odds against an unknown dog would be sky-high. Miguel could make a fortune.

But now Miguel's primary focus was on Elsie. After two months at sea and three pints of beer, she was, without doubt, the most beautiful woman he'd ever seen. McTavish knew that when this Guatemalan sailor left tonight with those orchid seeds, McTavish's chances of ever being rich would walk out with him. He must have those seeds. While lighting another cigarette from Miguel's cigar, the answer came to him.

Elsie wanted McTavish's magnificent *Hercules* bike but had no money. Miguel wanted Elsie and *Flash*, knowing that the greyhound was potentially a huge moneymaker.

McTavish beckoned to Elsie, wrapped his arm around her shoulder, and whispered into her ear. She recoiled, red-faced, before stomping angrily away. Faking tears, she wiped her hands on her towel, and then tossed it in the sink. Glaring at McTavish, she mouthed, "Disgusting swine."

Twenty minutes later, McTavish waved and smiled at her. Elsie blushed, before grinning back. He gestured to her with his thumb toward the pub's side-door then headed outside. A moment later Elsie followed, for one more look at the bike of her dreams.

By closing time, as the pub's owner flicked the lights on and off while calling, "Drink up folks," McTavish had closed his deal with Elsie and Miguel.

The next day Elsie was the proud owner of the magnificent *Hercules* bike. *Flash,* became the most famous greyhound in Venezuelan dog racing. Miguel had renamed him *Relampago*, which means lightning. In addition to fame, Miguel became quite rich.

McTavish was delighted with his five orchid seeds. Each seed grew well in its own red-clay pot. They received the special care described in an orchid book from the local library. The plants thrived in the warm sun which streamed through McTavish's kitchen window. Each noon, the lady from next-door stopped by to move them to his living room so they'd enjoy the afternoon sun. She even left the radio playing for them.

Three months later they were luxuriant, robust plants which McTavish and his neighbor were well pleased with.

Then, suddenly, and with no explanation, McTavish stopped visiting *The Galley.* The rumor was that he'd moved to Canada, Australia, or New Zealand. No one knew where, or even why.

All the guys in *The Galley* thought it was because he couldn't take a joke. Especially when the story got around about the deal McTavish made for *five cucumber seeds.*

PURPLE MAN

"THE OL' GUY'S CRAZY. HE must be. What's with his love of purple?" Josh asked his friend Brad.

They were walking Fritz; Brad's German shepherd. The white raised-ranch house sat on three acres, a little back from their quiet country road. Three tall maples and an old hickory tree shaded it in summer. In winter they sheltered it from biting cold winds which whipped across Lake Ontario, two miles to their North.

Josh was right. Patches of purple were everywhere. With his long black hair, his muscle shirt showing his tattoos, Josh was the cool one. He bounced as he walked, his head held high, self confidant.

"Who'd pick purple for the front door and shutters, on a white house? And all those purple flowers . . . yuk," Josh mocked.

Violets spread in great swaths around the maple's roots. The scent of Lilacs mixed with that of nodding purple iris, drifted on the gentle breeze. Bees buzzed around a hanging basket of purple lobelia on the front porch. Wide drifts of wood hyacinths, better known as bluebells, waved in the surrounding woods.

"Even his beat-up old Chevy's purple," Josh said, grinning "What's the word for freaky old guys who act weird?" he asked.

" Eccentric?" Brad offered.

"Yeah, that's it."

Brad was tall and wore glasses. His hair was short, probably because his dad was an ex-marine. Brad was the thinker, the book lover, much slower to judge.

No-one liked purple. It was for funerals, royalty or something. They'd once driven through the Southern Tier of upstate New York and laughed at the fire hydrants painted purple. It was because it was wine country with vineyards everywhere. The locals were pushing their wine, grape pies and stuff.

"Maybe he's found a good buy on a hundred gallons of that paint?" Brad said.

Whenever they walked Fritz after school, the same topic came up. One evening the old guy chugged by on his mower. He saw them and waved his floppy hat. His snow-white hair was stuffed under ear muffs. He wore a dark red work shirt and faded jeans. His John Deere mower was no longer the usual bright green. Now it was purple.

"What's happening Brad? Are we both in a weird dream? We've gotta change our route," Josh said.

Three days later Josh was sick and stayed home in bed. Brad walked Fritz alone. On that warm, July evening, Fritz barked, pulling and scaring a squirrel up the hickory tree in the purple man's front yard.

"Where's your friend tonight?" the old man asked, looking up from weeding by his front porch.

"He's sick." Brad replied. "Probably some kinda bug."

"Sorry to hear that. Would you tell him I was asking for him?"

"Thanks, I will," Brad said, standing while the old guy petted Fritz.

"Your friend's not big on purple is he?" the old man asked, smiling at Brad's puzzled glance. "How did I know?' the man asked, without waiting for a reply.

"On quiet evenings, voices carry, even when you're talking softly. I've heard your laughter and your friend joking at my shutters, flowers and truck. And that's okay, 'cause, I get it. I was a young guy once; sixty years back. When everything in life was funny, one long giggle, an endless party, with no worries. Every day was another big joke. They were wonderful days, a million laughs.

Then, suddenly I was old, and life swiveled around on me. One day, it kicked me hard; right in my gut," the old man said.

"Kicked you in the gut?" Brad repeated.

"Yeah. The day I lost my wife, my best friend, mother of our five children. The lady I've shared every day of my life for fifty-eight years. When that happened, I no longer wanted to live. I dreaded waking each morning because the loneliness squeezed my chest so hard that I could hardly breathe. But I had to force myself to get up, to soldier on, and do the best I could, "the old man said.

"You lost your wife?" Brad asked.

"Yes. It'll be five years next month. I had no hint, no warning. I never got chance to say goodbye or tell her I loved her. I awoke next to her and she was cold, already gone. Her name was Violet. We all called her Vi. No prize for guessing what her favorite color was," he said, smiling, through teary eyes.

"It's stupid I suppose, but now, purple comforts me. I feel close to her. As if she's with me, here in this yard."

He wiped his cheeks with the back of his hand. "None of this'll make any sense to you."

But he was wrong. For suddenly it did.

"Thanks for telling me this," Brad said, now understanding and feeling bad.

He began walking again, more slowly while inhaling the wonderful scent of lavender. It brought memories of his childhood naps at his grandma's. And her little bags of dried lavender which she stored with her linen. He knew that it must be growing somewhere in the old man's garden.

Brad continued, but slower now to Josh's house. Fritz was still pulling, and sniffing at every tree, glancing upward for squirrels.

Brad was suddenly older and wiser somehow. He was anxious to tell Josh of his epiphany.

"I'd better scratch *that word*. Josh hates big words. I'll just tell him that . . . the old guy's really cool," Brad explained to Fritz, who wasn't really listening.

RICH UNCLE JAKE

BACK IN 1980 WE ALL figured out that Uncle Jake was rich. He never actually told us that he was. We just knew it because of the signs we picked up on. He wasn't one for driving a Cadillac, smoking big cigars or wearing fancy clothes. In fact he was just the opposite. He was stingy, 'tight with the buck,' everyone whispered. Our family never actually said that, we just joked about his, 'saving for a rainy day.' 'The old miser has been saving since he was knee-high to a grasshopper,' Uncle Amos whispered about his older, seventy-eight year-old brother. Uncle Jake scrimped and mooched off everyone, while living alone in his draughty old cabin with the leaky roof, and bad plumbing. Finally, with arthritic hips, and a hacking cough from the smoky old woodstove, it became too much. He moved in with Maggie his niece, her husband and their four children. He wasn't the easiest person to live with. Maggie's kids thought that he looked like Rip Van Winkle with his pure white, shoulder length hair, and his long straggly beard. Persuading him to bathe was no picnic either.

During his fifteen years of courting the widow Jones, he'd bathe at her home on the nights she cooked his favorite meals. She even gave him haircuts and trimmed his beard. Once in a great while he took her to a movie and bought pizza. But that was years ago. Finally she'd given up on him, having realized that marriage wasn't in Jake's plans and their romance had no future. He hadn't cut his hair since and his old cowboy boots had never known polish.

He now spent his summer days rocking on his front porch, reading his Wall Street Journal puffing on his pipe and swatting flies.

"How yah doin' Uncle Jake?" children would call to him while passing back and forth to school. He'd lower his Wall Street Journal, peer over his glasses, grin, wave, and return to his paper.

He never bought that paper. Each morning he'd hobble down the street and scrounged it from Charlie's Diner. He rarely bought anything that he could borrow or get for free. That's how we figured he was rich. He mooched off everyone, and knew about stocks and shares.

We all believed that he owned an island, too. It was someplace warm, we figured, in the Caribbean or South Pacific. After a glass or two of his white lightning, he'd ramble on about his adventures.

At sixteen he'd left home, and hitched a truck ride to Massachusetts. He'd lied about his age, hired on as a deckhand on a merchant ship bound for Europe. On his seventeenth birthday he was torpedoed by a German U- boat in the Mediterranean. A Greek fisherman had dragged him half alive from the sea. Once recovered, he signed onto a freighter sailing through the Suez Canal to Australia.

We lost count of the all the places he'd visited. Uncle Amos told us they were all 'bull-ship' stories. Whatever kind of ships they were, they sounded pretty exciting to us kids.

Uncle Jake made hooch behind his barn. It was made from his secret recipe of corn, potatoes and honey. His buddies claimed you could run tractors on the stuff. Uncle would laugh and tell us it was mead. Hooch which the ancient Britons invented. After drinking the stuff those cave-men with painted faces and dressed in animal skins tossed the invading Roman army back into the English Channel.

After two glasses of his 'white lightning,' Uncle Jake would tell about adventures on his island. With slurred words, he'd ramble on about clean white beaches, swimming in the crystal clear lagoon, coconut palms and wild pigs running around. Apparently he'd lived there when he was young with his three pals. He never told us where it was or how he came to live on the island. It was just another of Uncle Jake's mysteries.

A few of our nosier relatives wondered where his island was. More importantly, did he own it outright? How much was it worth? And where had Uncle Jake hidden the deed?

"It's gotta be worth millions today," they whispered. They pictured cruise ships stopping by with lines of passengers buying souvenirs, straw hats, sunglasses and conch shells.

Uncle Jake had never earned much money. Mostly he'd worked on local farms doing odd jobs. Of course he never spent much either and still drove the rusty old '57 Chevy truck he'd bought way back when. Amazingly, after spluttering for a while, the old rust bucket still ran pretty good; considering it was held together with bits of wire.

'Your Uncle Jake squeezes a nickel so tight, the buffalo craps,' Uncle Amos would chuckle.

Everyone joked about Uncle Jake being cheap but he didn't mind. He'd just sit there smiling. We figured that was because he was rich and we weren't. He didn't just smile; often he'd giggle, as if enjoying a joke only he understood.

He once made a walking stick out of a gnarled hickory branch he'd found in the woods. We joked that Uncle Jake liked that dried-up twisted, stick because it matched his personality.

People were always analyzing his behavior to better understand him. We all wanted to learn where his wealth was hidden. Everyone denied this of course, pretending they had no interest in his money. But if Uncle Jake was ever missing, whenever our family got together for Thanksgiving, weddings and funerals, the subject of his money always cropped up. Everyone worried about his will. Had he made one? Was it hidden someplace? Who'd inherit most of it?

No one wanted to anger him in case he cut them out. Or maybe a family member would get too close, and become his favorite. He might then leave them his island, or half a million dollars.

Meanwhile Uncle Jake went quietly about his business, rocking on the front porch while puffing on his corn-cob pipe. Usually one of his grandkids would hang around, to swat flies for him or bring him a cold glass of lemonade.

Then, one hot, dusty, summer afternoon, Uncle Jake's chair stopped rocking. His corncob pipe dropped with a clatter, his newspaper crumpled in his lap, and Uncle Jake was gone; as quick as that.

Within hours the family began swarming. They came by car, truck, train, bus, horse and buggy. It was a really nice funeral with folks saying nice things about him. Later we ate barbecued pork, chicken, corn, sweet potatoes, fruit pies and jello. Uncle Amos found a few bottles of Uncle Jake's hooch in the cellar.

They searched for days and never found a will. They did find a few shares of General Motors, Eastman Kodak and Xerox stock. At one time they were worth a lot, but now they hardly paid for his funeral.

Uncle Jake did leave us with a few big surprises.

He had a very old, dusty book tucked away in his bedside table. Written inside the front cover was, 'To Jake on your Tenth Birthday, Love Mom and Dad'. The book was *Coral Island* by R.M. Ballantyne. It was an adventure story about three teenage boys, Jack, Peterkin and Ralph who were shipwrecked on a Polynesian island.

Then, shortly before Christmas, a large manila envelope arrived for Maggie, his niece, and his lady friend, the widow Jones. They were from Uncle Jake's lawyer and held the deeds for the homes they rented. Maggie and the widow Jones were now the new owners. Their mortgages had been paid in full, Uncle Jake's simple way of saying thank you. He'd instructed his lawyer to buy them after selling shares he'd bought years earlier in a small, risky, start-up company, named *Microsoft*.

He hadn't forgotten his brother Amos either who now was the proud owner of an old, but still reliable, '57 Chevy pick-up.

Oh yes, I almost forgot. He also left Amos a coffee can full of very old buffalo nickels. Each coin was carefully wrapped in tissue paper. *All were uncirculated, and in mint-perfect condition.*

They were worth considerably more than the old Chevy.

SHELL GAME

I T BEGAN WITH IMAGES FLASHING in my head, like a scene from a long forgotten movie.

I had boiled eggs to make a salad, but made too many. I peeled one and began eating it. The next I knew, I was standing in a long barn-like building. Around me were thousands of chickens in batteries of wire cages. The loud incessant clucking of chickens, along with the whirring of electric fans was deafening. The smell of ammonia and chicken droppings made me nauseous. Then, just as quickly I was back in my kitchen. Confused and feeling sick, I tossed my half-eaten egg into the trash. The sudden weird event really bothered me. The scene kept playing over and over in my head like a tune I'd heard on the radio.

Nights later, while enjoying a glass of wine with friends, a similar thing happened. While telling a joke I stopped in mid sentence. I felt suddenly dizzy, there was a flash of light and I was walking through a vineyard. The area was one which I recognized in the *Southern Tier of New York State*. We'd visited the vineyard the previous fall. Now it was a hot, late summer day and the vines were lush and heavy with grapes. The air was humid and smelled of sweet wine. A recent rain had left the ground spongy underfoot. There was a distant chatter of workers moving along the rows. From the distant woods a chain saw buzzed.

Then, just as quickly my dream faded and I was back with my wife and friends. I was telling my same old joke. But with the punch line, no one laughed. They just sat staring at me. They told me that I'd stopped talking in mid-sentence for two minutes while staring ahead as if in a trance. Then, I had blinked a few times before continuing from the very same point as if nothing had happened. I was too embarrassed to describe my dream. There was no feasible explanation so I blamed the wine, knowing that it was a lame excuse. Later, I checked the labels on our wine bottles and noticed they were bottled in vineyards in *New York's southern tier.* It was all too weird, especially when I remembered my 'boiled egg, chicken farm,' incident.

For a while my life at work, helping with the boy's homework and chores around the house was pretty uneventful.

Then, one Friday evening I took my family out for a fish-fry at our local diner. We chatted about school sports stuff and the tree house which the boys were building. I ordered my cod broiled for a change. Suddenly, I felt the ground heaving, pitching, and rolling. I stood up and leaned forward, gripping tightly onto the handrails of a fishing trawler. Beside me five burly fishermen in heavy yellow oilskins and knee-high rubber boots hauled bulging nets of cod aboard. I was drenched from the sea's freezing, lashing spray. The salty, biting wind sucked the breath from my lungs. I turned so that I could breathe easier, slipped and pitched sideways. While sliding down the sloping, sea-swamped deck, I tried grabbing for the rail.

Deep blackness faded before becoming gradually brighter. I looked up into my wife's face as she knelt beside me. Two puzzled waiters stared down at me.

"Are you okay?" they asked, while helping me to my chair.

"You grabbed for the table before falling sideways," my wife explained.

"You scared us," the boys said together. "We weren't sure if you were choking or just having a heart attack."

"Just a heart attack?" I quipped, trying to make light of it.

We finished our meal in awkward silence. I offered no explanation, knowing that I needed to meet with a doctor or a shrink. Whatever *this was*, it wasn't going away. I'd never heard of nightmares while folk were awake. It could happen at work or while driving. I wondered if a brain tumor might cause these things. My stress level wasn't bad, either at work or at home.

During dinner next day, Scot, our sandy haired eleven-year-old son, made an odd comment.

"Maybe you should've bought that necklace," Scot said, grinning.

"Necklace?" I asked.

"Yeah, remember last month, on our vacation? That wrinkled, old black woman with the long white hair and Jamaican accent, Scot said. "She was selling all kinds of junky stuff at that flea market in South Carolina."

"Who could forget her," I grinned. "She wanted a hundred bucks for a crappy necklace made from painted sea shells."

"Remember your laughing at her," Scot said, "and teasing her, saying, 'In your dreams lady', "while you and mom walked away?" Scot said.

"Yes, I remember," I said, swapping glances with my wife.

"Well, she didn't like you mocking her with your comment, 'in your dreams lady.' As you walked away she squinted her eyes into a mean, scary look. Then she leaned forward and pressed her face close to mine," Scot continued, repeating the black woman's words. 'Your papa he laughs now. But he no laugh in the coming days. He gonna wish he bought my seashell necklace,' Scot said, imitating her Jamaican accent.

'Dem seashells gonna look real pretty good 'round your momma's neck when her birthday come on June twenty,' Scot said. "But 'til your papa buy my seashell necklace, he have real bad dreams.'

"When did she say all this," I asked.

"Right after you and mom walked away. I was shaking one of her dried gourds. It had seeds in it and rattled like a maraca in a Mexican band."

I glanced from my wife to both boys.

"Who told her that your mom's birthday was on June twentieth?" I asked. They glanced at each other, and then shrugged in silence.

"Who told her?" I asked again, with still no answer.

"Someone must've told her." I insisted. "How else could she know?"

"Maybe she's a witch," Scot offered, grinning.

"Or a voodoo priestess," Bobbie, his older brother added, while elbowing Scot in the ribs.

"What else did the old woman say?" I asked of Scot.

"She said, 'After his bad dreams come; den he come back and buy dat necklace'."

Two days later, my wife and boys were enjoying ice cream for desert. I drizzled honey over my yogurt.

A sudden flash, the room spun, and I was ten-years-old again. I was dressed in shorts, a tee shirt, and sneakers while steadying a twelve-foot ladder for my granddad. He stood near the top, wafting smoke into a wild bee's nest which hung under the eaves of his cottage roof. His plan was to drop the nest into the sack he held beneath it. But the nest swung sideways and fell. It bounced off a rung of the ladder and landed by my feet. In seconds, hundreds of angry bees buzzed around my face, head, and neck. I ran, yelling while trying to escape from the hot, stinging needles of pain. Finally I dropped, curled up, with my arms around my head, sure that I was going to die. My nightmare ended as abruptly as it began.

"What's wrong with you?" my wife asked, crouching beside me, her arms around my shoulders. "You're here, safe with us," she said. "There are no bees. We're inside our home."

The next day I packed a few clothes before hugging, then waving goodbye to my family. I began the long, boring, eight-hundred-mile drive south. My wife had insisted that she really wanted *that seashell necklace* for her coming birthday.

SMALL GAME

OUR OLD FRIENDS BARNEY AND Janet were visiting us from New York City. They were anxious to see our newly built raised ranch. We gave them a tour of our home while catching up on their latest news. We reminisced about old times and the friends we hadn't seen for years. Barney and Janet were our age, in our late forties. Barney was tall, slim, with thinning hair, conservative and serious. Janet was attractive, a little heavy, outgoing and bubbly.

We were playing cards at the dining table, enjoying after-dinner Manhattans. It was then that we all saw it. A large, gray mouse flashed across the living room then under the sofa.

"Was that a mouse?" my wife asked, both surprised and embarrassed.

"Yes," we replied in unison, all of us having seen it.

"But we don't have any mice," my wife offered weakly.

"Well, obviously *we have one*," I replied, before jumping up and grabbing my air rifle from our hall closet. I loaded it with a lead pellet, and pumped it a few times.

"You can't be serious," my wife said, convinced that I was nuts. It made perfect sense to me. We had an unwelcome wild creature in the house. Being that I was a crack shot, I could quickly get rid of it.

"Quick Barney, grab one end of the sofa and raise it slowly," I yelled, first kneeling and then dropping quickly onto my stomach with my rifle aimed toward the sofa's underside.

"Is he always like this?" his wife asked mine in disbelief as Barney bent his knees and began lifting.

"After a few manhattans, anything's possible," my wife replied, watching as the sofa tilted upward. The mouse scurried out and our wives screamed. I fired but missed. The mouse streaked down our hallway before disappearing under our closed bathroom door.

"Shush," I yelled to the squealing ladies, afraid they'd awaken our three small children. As we trotted after our quarry down the hallway, I reloaded my rifle, then pumped it a few times. With sudden forethought, I grabbed a white, plastic toy bowling pin from our daughter's bedroom.

"It'll serve as a club in case I miss it again," I explained, then lay prone once more. My rifle was now aimed into the bathroom with the bowling pin lying by my right hand.

"Okay Barney, open the door slowly then flick on the light so I can see my quarry. The switch is to the left of the doorway"

"*Your quarry?*" my wife repeated, giggling as our wives' wrapped their arms around each other to console themselves on having such immature husbands. They doubted we should drink manhattans, or even strong coffee.

The door creaked slowly open as Barney snapped on the light. The mouse huddled in the corner, his ears were raised and his large black eyes stared straight into mine. I fired but missed him by a quarter inch. My pellet pinged into the baseboard as the mouse charged straight at me. Dropping my rifle, I grabbed the bowling pin and whacked him the instant he passed to my right.

"Unbelievable," Barney said, clapping his hands overhead and dancing like a running back having scored a touchdown at the Super Bowl.

"No one will ever believe all this back in the city. It's like being on a big game hunt on African Safari. Quick, feel my heart. It's about to jump clean out of my chest. God this was exciting. Did you guys plan this whole thing?" he asked.

"Plan it? Are you kidding me?" my wife asked. "Ever know him to plan anything? He's all, knee jerk reactions," she said, her tone flat, hinting of boredom, perhaps even despair.

"Everything's on pure impulse with him. You've known him long enough. By now you must know that he's crazy?" she said smiling, while glancing my way with obvious affection.

Meanwhile, Barney and Janet stood gazing silently down in wonderment, at my gray, very flat, trophy mouse.

A TRIP IN THE FALL

"YOUR AUNT PIGGY FELL OVER the dog," Uncle Amos said, laughing in that deep, mocking, belly laugh that everyone found so annoying. Luckily she'd only bruised her knees. My Aunt's name was Peggy but her husband, our Uncle Amos, called her Piggy. He thought it was funny but we found it mean. Especially because she was fifty pounds overweight and sensitive about it. Uncle Amos had a cruel streak and enjoyed teasing her. Whenever he laughed, he snorted like an old hog. We found him to be a most unpleasant man.

"He probably lies awake nights thinking of ways to tick us off," Jan, my fourteen-year-old sister said of him.

"Either he has a weird sense of humor, or he's trying to make the *Guinness Book of Records* as the world's biggest pain in the ass?" she added. It was true that no one liked him.

He was tall, round-shouldered, and skinny with an unruly mop of white hair. His hair stuck up and stayed there all day as if he'd sprayed it with lacquer. His teeth were stained brown from puffing on his corncob pipe. He smelled of tobacco and sweat because he rarely bathed. His jeans were torn and food-stains trailed down the front of his old brown shirt.

He wore old muddy sneakers during the hot months and cowboy boots when the weather cooled. The leather sole was loose on his left boot so that it flapped as he walked. He had to lift his foot higher with each step so he didn't trip over it. As he walked he waddled, clomping along like a penguin. Jan was embarrassed and ashamed when walking with him through the village.

"Everyone's staring," she complained.

"Who cares," he replied, grinning, with his left sole flapping as he swayed from side to side. Jan blushed, her head held down, wanting to crawl under a nearby bush.

"Don't worry what people think? They're all ignoramuses," Uncle Amos said. He liked that word and used it a lot. Jan didn't know what it meant until a year later. We figured he must be pretty smart, knowing those big words. But we still didn't like him.

Jan and I always felt sorry for Aunt Peggy because Uncle Amos treated her so mean. Our aunt was short and jolly with red chubby cheeks and long, snow-white hair which was always neat and rolled into a bun.

No one understood why aunt stayed with Amos. He wasn't loving, caring, or fun to be with. Jan and I saw him only as a mean, miserable, smelly old man, bent on tormenting everyone. Even their dog Moll avoided him, which says a lot because old dogs usually love you no matter what.

Never once did Aunt Peggy complain about her husband. She didn't fuss when he complained about his coffee being cold, or there wasn't enough milk or sugar, or that she hadn't stirred it. We never saw her angry, not even when he called her fat and ugly. Or, that her hair was a mess and the house a pigpen. She didn't even say anything when he forgot her birthday.

One Christmas she gave Uncle Amos a beautiful blue woolen cardigan which she'd knitted for him. He examined it for a moment, muttered that it was 'too big,' and then tossed it into the dog's basket.

When their male golden retriever was still a puppy he named it Molly. He knew the pup was a male, but he deliberately chose a girl's name because of his sick sense of humor. Even Molly disliked him. We figured that even the puppy knew that he was a male and that Molly was a girl's name. When Amos called, 'Come Molly,' he ignored him.

'That dog's so dumb he don't even know his name," Uncle Amos said. But Molly knew alright, he just didn't like Uncle Amos.

It was at the end of that long, sweltering summer that Uncle Amos met with his fatal accident.

He and Aunt Peggy were visiting Uncle Amos' brother in upstate New York. Close by was Letchworth State Park. It was known as the 'Grand Canyon of the East' because of the thousands of acres of magnificent scenery. As well as having impressive waterfalls it has very deep gorges. One gorge is five hundred feet deep. Uncle Amos was anxious to use the fancy camera Aunt Peggy gave him for his Birthday.

After his funeral Aunt Peggy told us more about Uncle Amos' awful fatal accident.

"He was taking pictures with his new digital camera," she said.

"It was a crisp, sunny afternoon in mid-fall. The trees were at their spectacular best in every shade of crimson, purple and gold. Your uncle loved waterfalls and the gorge has the highest one in New York State. He was determined to take a great picture. He walked over to the wooden fence while still peering down into his camera's viewfinder. Only Minutes earlier he'd yelled at Molly for barking and running back and forth at a squirrel in a nearby tree.

"Your uncle was walking slowly beside a low fence by the gorge's edge," Aunt Peggy whispered.

"One moment he was taking pictures. The next, he tripped over Molly and fell clean over the fence. It was terrible. Your uncle screamed all the way down," she said, wiping her eyes with a tissue, though they seemed dry to us.

A nearby Park Ranger heard uncle's terrifying scream of, "B- - - i - - -t - - -c - - - h," as he fell. Your uncle's loud cry while falling, echoed throughout the gorge.

By the time the breathless Park Ranger arrived at the scene, Molly was already locked back in the car.

"I was hysterical," Aunt Peggy whimpered. We couldn't see down into that five hundred feet deep gorge because of the thick shrubbery at the edge," aunt said.

'The ranger was wonderful. He phoned for the rescue squad, and then comforted me."

"So your husband was taking pictures and fell over Molly, your dog?" the ranger repeated as he took careful notes.

"Yes," Aunt Peggy said, answering all his questions, understanding their importance. The Ranger didn't check Molly very closely. If he had, he would have noticed that Molly was a male. He then may have questioned uncle's final scream.

"How did Uncle Amos fall?" we asked again, still puzzled, as Molly jumped at our knees, his tail whipping back and forth. We were trying to console Aunt Polly, who was dressed all in black, fresh from uncle's funeral. Still grieving and clearly upset she spoke slowly, choosing her words very carefully. "Well," she said, speaking softly, with a faint smile and a slight twitch in one eye, "Your uncle . . . fell over the dog."

WATER OTTER

W HEN I WAS TEN, MY Uncle Jack and Aunt Annie owned a pub in England. Uncle Jack was tall, skinny and close to sixty. What little hair he had was pure white and combed over to cover his almost baldhead. He wore wire-rimmed glasses which hung low on his nose. During my school's summer holidays I loved to visit for three weeks. Their place seemed always filled with colorful characters which practically lived in their pub. When it was closed, I'd pretend to play their piano and plunk away for hours. When tired of that, I'd move over to the dartboard.

Uncle Jack was my favorite because he was jokester and great fun to be around. He loved to tease, was rarely serious and had a zillion funny stories. He poked fun at his unsuspecting customers while keeping a straight face. He led them along paths of unbelievable fantasy. Even as a young lad, I knew when he was pulling someone's leg. I'd watch with fascination as my uncle conned his unsuspecting patrons. His accent was broad Cheshire and was so hard to understand, it was barely English.

Rodney, Uncle Jack's favorite victim, was a bit slow. Many pub customers whispered that he was, 'as daft as a brush.' It was pretty mean, but after a few pints of beer, Englishmen are not the kindest or gentlest of folk.

Though slow, Rodney was a helpful, lovable young man in his late twenties. He wore thick goofy glasses, a brown floppy tweed cap, and a green woolen sweater which had shrunk and was now much too small. His grey pants were baggy with blotches of dried white paint from a recent job.

Rodney liked Uncle Jack and was quick to help with odd jobs around the pub. Uncle would slip him a few shillings for beer money. Sadly, my uncle couldn't resist teasing him unmercifully.

"Hey Rodney; 'as thee heard about the old, black water otter I just caught down at yon barge canal?" my uncle asked him one afternoon.

"No Jack, I 'aven't heard."

"Well, he's a 'uge, black ugly bugger. It's down in my beer cellar on an 'eavy chain. Would thee like to see 'im?"

"Aye, Jack I would . . . but will it bite me? Is it dangerous?"

"'Course its bloody dangerous? Them water otters are real savage, ferocious buggers. You wouldn't want 'im grabbin' onto your leg. He'd drag you around and rip it off in a minute with 'is 'uge sharp teeth. You'd better take this flashlight Rodney. The light bulbs burned out down inth cellar. Follow me lad and mind these old slippery wooden stairs. They're real steep and rickety. Grab onto the 'and rail and keep a sharp eye open for that bloody otter."

"Jeez Jack, I'm scared.' 'Ow big is it? It's real cold and dark down 'ere Jack. I can't see much . . . where is it?"

"It's 'iding over there, under them big wooden beer barrels. 'Ere Rodney, shine your light on its 'eavy chain on the dirt floor. I'll just give it a big yank."

"Ooh I'm shakin' Jack. Look, my knees are knockin'. I'm afeared. You won't let 'im get me will you Jack?"

Uncle Jack gave a sudden, hard tug. Then out it came with a loud, tumbling, clanking, clattering, and rolling. It was a rusty, black iron kettle. Rodney screamed, jumping backwards while dropping his flashlight, then frantically scrambling halfway up the wooden stairs. Below him, now in total darkness, Uncle Jack howled with laughter while slapping his knees and doubled over.

"Did you see it Rodney? Uncle Jack asked, calling to Rodney who was still whimpering while scrambling frantically upward, still on hands and knees.

"I fished this old water 'otter out of the barge canal," uncle said.

"When I was a young lad, we 'ad one just like it. My job every mornin' was to fill it wi' water, then 'ang it over the fire. Back in them old days, that's 'ow we 'otted our water."

WORDS TO LIVE BY

S AM WAS A HOPELESS BIBLIOPHILE, obsessed with books. As a child he had only three books because his family was poor. Now in his mid-seventies, he still treasured those same three books, among many, many more.

He was eight when his mom took him for his library card. After that, whenever he borrowed books it felt like Christmas. Even now, whenever his local library had a book sale, he'd bring home a bag full. His wife was afraid that one day their house would collapse, but that didn't stop him. Books had always been special, in fact, when just a young man, *one had saved his life.*

In Britain in the late forties, when eleven, all children sat for a written examination. Those who passed went to High School, those who failed, attended Secondary Schools. Being either nervous or dumb, Sam had failed. His only option was to enroll at a nearby Secondary School for Boys. High School students graduated when eighteen, Secondary School students finished school when fifteen. Britain viewed these as less bright and better suited for the lower positions of the workforce.

Sam liked his teachers. They managed to instill pride and ambition in their students. Failing his earlier test had a positive effect. It stimulated his desire for knowledge. Four years later he was the top student in his graduation class of a hundred and forty. Learning a trade was typical for non-high school kids. Sam began a six-year engineering apprenticeship with one of Britain's top companies. After work, on three evenings each week he studied technical classes. At twenty-four, with his apprenticeship completed, he married, and brought his new wife to the States. He worked beside brilliant engineers where technology was ever advancing. He knew that he must keep up with change or become a dinosaur. Years later, when asked, 'Are you mechanical or electrical?' he smiled, for by now he was proficient in both.

Mechanical engineers specialized in small mechanisms, office copiers, printers, clocks, watches, or cameras. Some worked on heavy earth-moving equipment, bulldozers, hydraulics, and structures for bridges and tall buildings. Electrical engineers specialized in electronics, heating, power generation, distribution, and motors. Areas, such as automotive, marine, military, chemical, and medical, often required that engineers be experienced in both. When Sam needed technical data, the library was always there. It was his ever-loyal friend, helping him provide for his family.

One afternoon, as Sam returned with an arm full of books from the library, Bert, his teenage grandson grinned, while nudging Maggie, his younger cousin.

"Grandpa's losing it," he whispered, just loud enough for Sam to hear.

"Why would you say that?" Sam asked.

"Because gramps," Bert explained, "books are obsolete. Who reads 'em anymore? Everything you need is on your computer."

There was some truth in what Bert said, but he didn't know that his gramps had helped design the early computers. That was back in the early sixties when he was a consultant engineer with such companies as IBM, ITT, GE, and the U.S. Military.

Bert's words, 'Books are obsolete,' had stung, raising painful memories of a half-century earlier. When eighteen, Sam sat reading a book on an English mountaintop. The wind had turned the pages on the book which saved his life. If *that book* had been Bert's precious *Kindle,* neither Sam nor Bert would be alive.

Sam was an apprentice, earning eight dollars for a forty hours work. He worked overtime, while attending classes on three nights each week. On two nights he attended Judo classes. Each Saturdays he worked twelve hours on his second job. After homework there was little time for fun or sleep. It was not surprising that he suffered from exhaustion, impatience and carelessness.

Soon after his eighteenth Birthday, one bitter cold winter's morning, during his train ride to work, Sam's compartment door froze closed. When at his station, in his effort to exit, he shouldered the door frame and shattered the plate-glass window. He severed four tendons in his right hand and almost bled to death. After surgery, he learned that he may lose the use of his right hand. He could think of only two jobs which a one-handed man might do, an elevator operator, and a floor sweeper. Being eighteen, poor and friendless, with his job prospects now very bleak, Sam sank into deep depression. He questioned the point of living. It was the lowest, darkest period of his young life.

One Sunday morning in the late autumn, he decided that he couldn't go on. With his right hand in a cast and a sling, he struggled to dress. His mother packed his lunch, and then helped tie his boots. By pure chance, she slipped the book that his friend had loaned him into her son's pack. It was *'Doctor in the House,'* by Richard Gordon.

"Take care Sam," his mother whispered as she kissed him goodbye, adding quickly, "I wish you wouldn't hike alone."

"I'll be fine mom," he said, feeling bad for lying to her.

He first caught a bus, then a train to Edale, in the High Peak District of Derbyshire. He climbed slowly up the long, steep, winding trail to Mount Kinder Scout. It was a place he knew well having hiked and climbed there many times with friends. While trudging up the rock-strewn mountain pass, the cold damp biting wind whipped through his anorak. With his right arm in a sling, hiking was tricky. If he were to slip he'd instinctively reach forward with both hands to break his fall. Feeling helpless and vulnerable, he kept going, determined to reach the waterfall, known as *The Downfall.* When frozen, it was popular with ice climbers who practiced there. As Sam struggled up the slippery mountain pass, he gave little thought to his return trek. He planned on a *much quicker and shorter route.*

Huge granite crags jutted up through the grassy slopes where black-faced sheep grazed. High above, an eagle screeched while spiraling on the thermals. Farther up the trail a hare leapt up, bounced twice, and then was gone. In spite of the cold wind and light drizzle, Sam was sweating and breathing hard. His eyes were fixed on the mountain's peak and the jutting plateau overlooking the valley far below.

Finally he reached the mountain's peak and stood, leaning forward, his left hand braced on his knee, his chest heaving. The biting cold wind brought tears to his eyes. He admired the magnificent grandeur stretching to the far horizon. Below, the river shimmered as it snaked through the black-green valley. Sheep dotted the endless, rolling hills. Sam found it odd that there were no trees. It gave the landscape a stark, empty, lifeless appearance.

From the plateau, he looked down to the jagged rocks, like snarling teeth, four hundred feet below. After struggling to free his shoulders from his rucksack, he rummaged for his lunch. He was surprised to find the book which his mom had packed earlier.

"Now for a picnic," he said, smiling at the irony. With only one hand, his life would hardly 'be a picnic.'

"I'll eat first, read my book for half an hour, grab a few quick, deep breaths to psych. myself up . . . and then jump," he said aloud with little emotion as the wind snatched his words away.

Sam began reading his book. At random he chose the chapter describing a dramatic scene in Scotland. A young student doctor was tasked with delivering a baby. Both the mother and her baby were mannequins. This was very fortunate because the young trainee doctor was hung over from a party a few hours earlier. His Professor phoned him at 3:00 am. with an address where he was to perform a simulated childbirth. It was on an especially bitter cold, miserable winter's night. As the young doctor pedaled his bike, weaving along the dark empty streets, he worried that his professor might smell his breath. Finally, he reached the neglected, grey stone, apartment. Clutching his heavy black leather surgical bag, he climbed the two flights of creaking wooden stairs.

His professor led him into the dark, damp, sparsely furnished bedroom. A single kerosene lantern flickered, casting shadows on the polished wooden floor. A very pregnant mannequin lay on a bed. Beside it was an oval, braided, brown, and green, bedroom rug.

The student doctor washed his hands in freezing water, and then examined *the pregnant woman.* As he began the birthing procedure he was painfully aware of his professor's critical watch of his every move. Nothing was going well. Neither mother nor baby co-operated. Finally, in desperation, he selected his obstetrical tongs. He clamped them tenderly onto the baby's head then pulled, very gently at first. Then harder, but without success. His professor frowned. Now desperate and near panic, the student gave one last, mighty pull.

Suddenly, the bedside rug on which he stood slipped forward. His feet and legs shot under the bed as the mannequin mother somersaulted over his head. It crashed hard into the wall then lay in a twisted, crumpled heap. While lying on his back, half under her bed, he looked with horror at his obstetrical tongs in which was only the baby's head. At this nightmare moment, he stared up into his professor's angry face. His professor bent over him, his face distorted with disgust. He next offered him a heavy wooden mallet.

"Here," he hissed. "Smash the baby's father's skull with this and you will have killed the whole bloody family."

Sam snapped his book closed and let it fall into his lap.

Seconds elapsed. Then, very softly and slowly at first, he began to laugh. It was a sound that he hadn't made for two years. Exhausted from his work, school, and lack of sleep, he'd forgotten how to laugh. Now, he heard it bubbling up from somewhere deep within him. As if a bloated infected abscess had suddenly burst. His laughter grew gradually louder, finally becoming an uncontrollable maniacal cackle. Tears rolled down Sam's cheeks and his chest hurt. He cupped his face in his one good hand as his laughter turned into tears.

He then stood staring again to the rocks below and felt suddenly ashamed of his weakness and self-pity. He begged for God's forgiveness. For the strength and will to live, even if it meant life with only one hand.

A sudden gale-force wind pushed him backward, away from the cliff's edge. Sam took it as heaven's sign. He knelt and stuffed his thermos and now precious book into his rucksack before wriggling into the straps of his rucksack.

While heading back down the long rock strewn trail, he glanced up at the clouds. "Lord thank you for teaching me to laugh again," he said, his words snatched instantly away in the wind.

He waited on the railroad station's platform for his train home. Four hikers stood talking nearby, their rucksacks by their feet. Sam stared along the track at the approaching train, its steam belching into the darkening sky. The chugging, clanging steel giant slowed, and then stopped, its brakes hissing. The grinning fireman leaned out of his cab, waving his greasy black cap as the hikers grabbed their packs and scrambled aboard.

Before Sam reached for the door, he heard a strong, clear, gentle voice close behind him.

"Your hand will completely heal," the voice said. Sam spun around. He was alone on the platform.

"The remainder of your life will be rich and wonderful," the voice continued. "Don't ever waste it." Sam trembled, his eyes now suddenly wet, and his vision blurred with tears.

"Thank you Lord," he whispered, his words swept upward up with the hissing steam.

With his head held higher now and his pack somehow lighter, he waved his good hand to the fireman and climbed aboard.

BIRDMAN

A LAN PIGEON LOVED BIRDS OF all kinds. As a boy with red hair and a large nose, he'd been a perfect target for his school mates teasing. He didn't mind because he was good natured and easy going. When teased he'd just smile, then laugh right along with his tormentors who called him 'bird- brain, eagle beak,' or a 'red-headed Nut thatch.'

One early memory was of lying on his back in the tall ferns on a Scottish hillside. He watched as the clouds drifting overhead and seagulls swooped, crying while playing tag on the high winds. Since early childhood, birds had held a strange fascination for him.

One special day in 1948 when he was ten, his mother took him to visit an aunt. Alan hated visiting because it was boring. Grown-ups just sat around talking and drinking tea for hours. With nothing to do, he'd quickly grow bored. But this day was different. On a coffee table by a picture window overlooking his aunt's flower garden was a blue bird in a cage. It chirped loudly while swinging back and forth ringing its bell.

"What's that bird?" he asked, never having seen a pet bird up close before.

"That's Joey, our budgie," his aunt replied.

"Budgie?" Alan repeated.

"Yes, Budgie is short for Budgerigar, a parakeet. They came originally from Australia. Parakeet means small parrot and like parrots, they can talk."

"He can talk?" Alan asked, in disbelief, leaning forward, peering into Joey's cage.

"Yes," his aunt said. "Pull up a chair and sit with him. He'll talk to you."

Alan sat, watched and listened, little knowing the next hour would change his life forever. He became instantly hooked. Fascinated by that little blue bird which not only talked, but did tricks. Joey meanwhile, was so thrilled with having an audience; he hopped on his swing, rang his little bell, jumped to a lower perch, and admired himself in his mirror.

"Pretty Joey, pretty bird," Joey said, in small, but clear voice.

"Jack and Jill went up the hill," the bird said, as Alan sat wide-eyed, barely breathing.

"Hello grandma," Joey said finally. The bird had an assortment of tricks. A small, plastic, black and white toy policeman stood on the cage's sandy floor. Joey pecked hard at the doll's face. It wobbled wildly back and forth but didn't topple. Alan was amazed at the bird's performance and energy. Alan's mom couldn't believe that Alan had sat for a solid hour watching a bird.

"I've never known him quiet for so long," she'd said.

Ten days later she bought Alan a sky-blue budgie, a cage, mirror, bell, swing, and a plastic, policeman doll.

The bird had a necklace of black spots, and a long black tail. Alan also bought a book on Budgerigars. He needed to know everything about them. He learned the males made the best talkers.

"Unlike humans, eh," his grandpa said, winking as he spoke.

Each Saturday morning, Alan rode the 75 bus to Tib Street, in the heart of Manchester. The small street was unique in having four pet stores. Alan wandered wide-eyed through each store, admiring the puppies, rabbits, white mice, snakes, lizards, tortoises, tropical fish, canaries, and especially budgies. He bought seed, grit, cuttlebone, and other treats.

Mostly he needed a mate for his budgie so that he could breed them and sell babies. He joined the local Budgie club and dreamed of showing his birds. Alan's grandfather took him to a rabbit show. He learned that a local Budgie Club held an annual show. He wondered if he'd ever win a trophy with one of his birds. Years later Alan's dream came true, far beyond anything he could have imagined.

When he was eighteen he became secretary of The Manchester Budgerigar Society. At twenty-four he married and moved to the USA where he continued with his hobby. He entered two of his birds in a Show in Buffalo, where he won 'Best Bird in Show.' He began showing his birds in New York, Pennsylvania, Connecticut, Massachusetts, and Rhode Island. After winning thirty-five trophies, he became a 'Champion Breeder,' and began judging shows. He wrote articles for bird magazines and was guest speaker at clubs in the USA, Canada, Scotland, and Australia. For sixty years budgies were a major part of his life. Then, one very strange day his life changed dramatically.

He vaguely remembered falling onto the hard wooden floor of his bird room. The incident was cloudy and nagged at him for weeks. His recollection was fuzzy. 'Was it memory loss caused by a stroke,' he wondered.

His life now was vastly different. 'Where was he?' he asked himself while watching a white-haired, chubby man move slowly along a narrow aisle-way between walls lined with bird-cages. Budgies chattered loudly in their long wooden breeding cages which were stacked three-high from floor to ceiling. The loud, incessant chatter of a hundred budgies in many colors was familiar to him. He'd heard that sound most days of his life.

He watched, the man move from cage to cage putting fresh water in the glass-tube drinkers hooked on the cage-fronts. He blew seed husks from each dish before adding more canary, panicum millet seed, and oats. Finally, he clipped a millet spray onto the inside of each cage. Alan had followed this same procedure every morning in his own bird-room. The man continued, checking nest-boxes hanging on each cage's side. Any change inside a nest-box was noted on a card pinned to its side. He recorded when eggs were laid and when they should hatch. When a chick was seven days old, he slid a small metal band onto one leg. Each band carried data such as when it was hatched, the bird's number, and the identification code of the breeder. A bird could then be recognized as having been bred by this man. Alan had seen the same system used on his trips to Australia, New Zealand and Canada.

Alan recognized the man as Frank Morris. They'd met four years earlier in Massachusetts. Alan and Frank were both Champion Breeders and were competing for, the 'Best Bird in Show.' Frank had beaten Alan with a magnificent Lutino Hen. It was unusual for a pure yellow bird with pink eyes to win, Best Bird in Show. Usually the much larger Light-Greens won. Alan was disappointed that his, 'Best Champion Opaline Light-Green Hen' hadn't won. But in fairness, Frank's Lutino was truly magnificent and deserved the top award.

Now, Alan found himself in Frank Morris's bird-room watching as Frank moved steadily along, feeding, and checking nest-boxes.

'How did I get here?' Alan wondered again. The question he'd asked himself so many times over the past weeks. Ever since his severe memory jolt, the day he'd remembered his previous life. Since then he'd pieced his thoughts and half forgotten incidents together until finally he understood. He now realized he was neither crazy or living a nightmare. There was no logical explanation.

Incredible though it was, *Alan Pigeon was now a budgie,* complete with wings, *bright green feathers, beak, thin scaly legs and clawed feet. He also chirped, ate seed and could fly.*

He'd neither heard of such a thing nor believed it even possible. But there was no mistake; *Alan Pigeon was now a budgie.* He knew Frank Morris from a different time in a very different life.

Alan needed to forget those days, bury them, and accept this new his life.

His thoughts snapped back to that fateful, terrible day. *The day he'd died.*

He remembered moving from cage to cage, in his own bird-room. It was a week after his seventy-fifth birthday. He'd been in good health, enjoying retirement. On that day, he remembered feeling suddenly dizzy, the sudden stabbing pain in his chest, dropping his seed bucket, his knees buckling as he fell into empty blackness. He knew nothing more.

His memories, until a week ago were of growing up from a young bird.

Since then, he'd struggled to figure things out, to better understand. It had been a slow, gradual, tormenting realization of where he was and what had happened. He'd heard of re-incarnation. Of people coming back as another person or animal. What were the chances of his coming back as a budgie?

When he knew the truth, he tried attracting Frank Morris's attention, to let him know who he really was. He finally realized *it just wasn't possible.* There was no possible way that he could communicate his situation. Who'd believe such a thing? He, Alan Pigeon certainly wouldn't. It was, without doubt, the wildest, craziest, most amazing thing that anyone ever heard of. Yet, here he was. After weeks of wondering if he were crazy he'd finally given up and fallen into a state of acceptance and deep depression.

As Frank Morris drew nearer, Alan tapped his beak loudly on the cage bars and fluttered back and forth from perch to perch, chirping loudly. He needed to grab Frank's attention.

With luck, Frank would give him a piece of carrot.

JANE'S LAMP

JANE SAT DEEPLY ENGROSSED AT her kitchen table in her neat, cozy home in Huntsville Alabama. Her table was littered with an assortment of parts off the tall, black iron pole lamp which usually stood by her driveway. "What happened?" I asked.

"We had a horrendous wind storm which blew it off the post. There were pieces lying scattered all over the driveway," she explained. "Now I can't figure out which piece goes where."

"It should be easy to figure out," I offered, little realizing that my big mouth would win me the job.

"Not really," she said. "My husband Bill cobbled it together from spare parts he'd cannibalized from junk stuff, so nothing really fits together."

"Okay, let me take a shot. I should be able to figure it out," I said, rising to the challenge. Let's just say that her lamp wouldn't cooperate. Nothing fit together or even came close. Believing that determination is a powerful asset when faced with the seemingly impossible, I persisted. While struggling under everyone's gaze, I grew increasingly more embarrassed by my lack of progress.

"Try this," my wife suggested, pressing various bits together while leaning over my shoulder. Those parts continued to defy all my efforts to assemble them.

"Weren't you an engineer?" someone asked as I reached for the duct tape.

"Yes, I was. Thanks for pointing that out," I mumbled. 'Why is it that whenever I am struggling, I always have an audience?' I wondered.

"We're only trying to help you," my wife offered, grinning while relishing my struggle.

Eventually Jane's lamp was assembled and ready for mounting atop her seven-foot-high, black steel post in her front yard. I climbed her eight foot aluminum ladder and began examining the electric wiring. The bare copper wires still stood straight up as they had since the lamp housing was ripped away in that high wind.

Tommy, Jane's five year-old grandson who was blessed with the energy of a puppy on steroids. He raced tirelessly in and out of trees, bushes and around the base of my ladder. Let's say that when you're seventy-two and perched on top of a ladder, young boys running around the base of it hold your attention.

"Do you know which wall switch turns this lamp on?" I asked.

"Yes, this one," Jane assured me, pointing with absolute certainty to the one just inside the front foyer. I checked the wiring with my electric tester without success. There was power at the switch but none at the lamp. It made little sense. How could an underground power line have been cut during a wind storm?

After my climbing up and down that ladder half a dozen times, I had a lucky break. Dawn, Jane's daughter stopped by for a visit. "That's not the switch," she insisted." It's this one." She was right.

Both Jane and I felt pretty foolish. I couldn't believe that I hadn't thought to try different switches. In my defense, fifty years of marriage has conditioned me not to question authority.

Okay, so now we had power at the lamp post. We turned off the switch while I began mounting the heavy cast steel lamp on top of the post. While I'm twisting the electric wires together, balanced precariously near the top rung of an aluminum ladder, which stood in a pool of water on the lawn, I heard Dawn yell to her young son. "Don't turn that on!" Had Tommy thrown that switch; yours truly would have lit up like the proverbial Christmas tree. An aluminum ladder in water being an excellent electrical conductor. If Tommy had flicked on that light switch it would have had an interesting effect. I visualized blue sparks, a piercing scream and my falling backwards onto the lawn, with a large, heavy steel lamp lying on top of my charred, smoking very still body.

Fortunately my fear was unfounded because Tommy was only attempting to turn on the hose pipe, thank heavens. My sudden terror and panic attack had been without cause. My pulse rate dropped back to normal when I saw Tommy sitting quietly on the lawn swing, enjoying a dish of ice cream. I could now safely finish hooking up the wiring without fear of sudden death.

Once the lamp sat securely back on its post with all its screws tightened, I asked Jane to flick on the switch. Hey presto, it worked and cast a wonderful warm glow onto her lawn.

"It works. Amazing, my wife said. "Why so amazing?" I replied. "I was an engineer for over forty years."

"True, but then I've been married to you for forty-eight."

Just then a bee began showing great interest in my left nostril.

"Why is this bee buzzing around my nose?" I hollered.

"It's probably looking for a place to build a nest," my wife suggested.

I once swatted a bee when I was seven. I didn't kill it, but made it pretty mad. It must have passed the word around because since then its many cousins have been after me.

Between that bee attracted to my nostril and little Tommy trying first to knock me off the ladder and then electrocute me, I'm quite proud. Against such odds, I'm fortunate that Jane's lamp finally lit and was such a wonderful sight.

As a footnote; four years have since passed with a number of tornadoes having churned their destruction through Jane's section of Alabama. To date I'm *de-lighted* to report that the lamp still illuminates Jane's front lawn.

FATHER'S DAY

O N THIS VERY SPECIAL DAY we'd invited my dad for dinner. Not an ordinary every day dinner, but one which we hoped he'd always remember. Everything which my wife and I had prepared was home raised. There were sweet potatoes, mashed plain white ones, fresh picked corn, Brussels sprouts, and our *pie'ce de resistance,* a large roast goose. We even made plum wine from our plum tree, followed by rhubarb pie with thick, delicious custard.

Dad was especially thrilled because it was the first time he had visited our hundred and fifty year-old- farm house which sat on three acres surrounded by the tangled wild grape vines climbing the tall trees in our woods, and our small patch of orchard.

My wife and our three children were aiming for self sufficiency by growing our own vegetables, raising chickens and a few geese. We were pretty green, naiveté former city folks, overly optimistic without a clue about country life. We'd had disappointments to be sure, but viewed it as adventurous fun.

We sat chatting in our living room as my wife busied herself in the kitchen, among the tantalizing smells of roasting goose, the clatter of dishes and the hum of her electric mixer.

After months of planning and looking forward to this, my dad was finally here. He leaned back in his dining chair for a while with a look of wonderment. His gaze swept over the feast on our dinner table. And what a spread it was.

Dad said grace and then glanced down at his dinner. He reached first for the gravy and poured it slowly over his heap of white potatoes.

"Look kids, Mount Vesuvius is erupting," he said as the thick gravy trickled down his mountain of mashed potatoes. Our children grinned because their grandpa was a kidder, forever teasing them and playing tricks. They still giggled and whispered about the time he'd brought them a Whoopee Cushion.

Dad picked up his huge goose drumstick, turned it this way and that admiring its golden brown crispy meat which was cooked to perfection. He pushed his nose close to it and inhaled its rich smell before drawing it to his mouth and sinking his teeth deep into the moist flesh. He closed his eyes as the juice dribbled down his chin before he caught it with the napkin in his other hand. He moaned while chewing slowly, his eyes still closed, as he spoke in almost a whisper.

"So son, is it really true that you and Mary raised all this food on your wee farm?" dad asked.

"Aye dad, it's true, we did," I replied.

"It's amazing . . . hard to believe son. How many folk can ever claim to have raised all this themselves? It's truly amazing. But one thing puzzles me," he said.

"What's that?" I asked.

"This goose son. I thought you didn't like to kill anything?"

"It's true dad, I don't."

"But then how'd you kill this goose?"

"I poisoned it," I said.

Dad's eyes opened very wide and he stopped chewing. His drumstick shot an arm's length away from his lips. He stiffened and sat bolt upright in his chair. For three full minutes he neither spoke nor swallowed a morsel.

We couldn't contain ourselves a moment longer. My wife and I, along with all three children exploded into laughter.

When Dad finally realized that he'd been had, he risked swallowing, and began laughing along with us.

WAGAMBUTTI'S VILLAGE

FRED WAS BORED THE DAY he stopped by the travel agents and casually picked up a brochure of Papua, New Guinea. He had no intention of ever going there, or was even sure where it was. Still in his early twenties, he'd recently broken up with his girlfriend and needed to get away. He'd considered a cruise, but he had few friends and couldn't imagine going alone. But travelling to Papua, New Guinea . . . _that_ would be a real adventure. On his return he'd have something to brag about. Many have taken cruises, but who's been to New Guinea? It would be expensive, but so what. He rarely used his credit card and because of his small balance, he was in danger of losing it. So why not? If nothing else Fred was adventurous and impulsive. Nothing like his dad, the ever cautious New York City cop. Fred had three weeks' vacation due him. What the hell . . . he'd do it.

Two weeks later he stepped off the plane in Papua. The weather was glorious. The airport swarmed with laughing, tanned tourists in brightly colored cotton shirts, sandals, white shorts, loose dresses and floppy, wide-brimmed hats. Everyone was in a festive mood and why not? This had to be paradise. From the plane he'd gazed upon lagoons, mountains and endless forests surrounded by azure seas. He felt better already and he hadn't yet collected his luggage.

Through his travel agency he'd booked into a modest hotel. Though nothing fancy, it was clean, overlooked the ocean and had a swimming pool. On his first evening he sat sipping a Mai Tai on a palm-covered verandah beside the pool. He watched as the sun sank slowly behind distant tree-sloped mountains. He'd never seen such beauty. He felt blessed, knowing that surely, he'd found paradise.

From a nearby table shaded by a brightly colored umbrella, a dark-skinned native sat sipping on an exotic fruit drink. The man wore a floral Hawaiian shirt, white shorts and a hat with the side brim turned up Aussie style.

"May I join you? The native asked, smiling while walking over.

"Do you like these tourist places, or would you prefer to see *the real* New Guinea?"

"What's the difference?" Fred asked.

"Well there's tourist-trap souvenir shops, bars, and strip clubs. Or there's *the New Guinea,* which tourists *never see.* There is our Island of two-hundred-years ago. The one you'll only find in history books. For a hundred dollars I can show you *that real place.* The authentic, primitive world of native Papuans, unchanged from how it once was."

"Now *that* sounds really interesting," Fred said, as the dark-skinned man drew his chair closer while signaling for more drinks.

"My name's Wagambutti. My village is a three-hour journey over very rough roads. Your cell phone's useless but bring your camera to record your adventure, if you wish to visit."

"I'm in," Fred said, draining his glass and beckoning for two more.

They set out early next morning in Wagambutti's open jeep. They ate a fruit breakfast as they drove along, bouncing upward along the narrow, hard-clay mountain road. Trees and vines drooped low causing them to duck. Occasionally wild boar and goats darted across their trail and exotic birds chattered as they journeyed higher through the dense forest. Fred marveled at the magnificent sub-tropical scenery which he glimpsed through openings in the trees, then on to the pale-blue ocean, a thousand feet below. After a ninety minute, bumpy drive, they stopped by a small village. Seven naked native children screamed, splashed, jumped and giggled together in a pool fed by a thirty-foot waterfall. A dozen palm-covered wooden huts lay scattered around a clearing where chickens scratched, picking and kicking up dust. Sheep, goats and boney cows grazed inside a paddock surrounded by a crude, woven rush fence.

Wagambutti parked his jeep before chatting with a frail, old, dark-skinned native who then led two mules to Wagambutti. The old man might have stepped from the pages of a National Geographic magazine. His entire clothing was a strip of cow hide. A six-inch-long, white bone needle ran through his nose and his ear lobes were stretched with sea- shells. His cheeks were crisscrossed with white painted scars. The mules were so thin, their ribs were clearly visible. Wagambutti caught Fred's look of disbelief.

"My Jeep won't make the narrow mountain roads," he said before climbing onto his mule then waiting for Fred to follow. 'No-one's gonna believe any of this,' Fred thought as his mule plodded slowly up the rock-strewn winding track. Mosquitoes were ever-present, except on the rare occasions when the two men broke free of the dense trees and were suddenly in bright sunshine.

Thirst was their constant companion. Wagambutti passed Fred a canteen of fruit juice. It tasted like peach but was much stronger. It probably had alcohol, Fred decided. It certainly had a kick to it. 'If I keep drinking this I'll never last another hour,' he thought, feeling increasingly drowsy with the steady, rhythmic plodding of his mule's hooves. Once or twice he closed his eyes and was afraid he'd fall asleep. The fruit juice, heat and swaying mule were hypnotic.

Finally, at Wagambutti's village, four natives lifted Fred from his mule and laid him on a goatskin blanket. He remembered very little of this because he was heavily drugged.

When he awoke an hour later, he was lying on his back in the village clearing. His arms and ankles were chained to an eight-foot long, heavy steel pole. Above his head was a heavy crank for turning it. Fifty yards away, wood smoke drifted steadily upward from a ten-foot long, eighteen inch deep pit.

Native children chased each other around the pit, playing tag in the smoke, and whipping at each other with wet palm leaves. The villagers were in a festive mood. They wore colorful ceremonial dresses, cloaks and long skirts made of dyed skins. Their faces and limbs were daubed with mud and paint. Their hair was decorated with brightly colored bones, sea-shells and feathers. The women sat cross-legged while rattling gourds and beating drums. Their men chanted while dancing a slow, high stepping dance and blowing on conch shells.

At each end of the smoking pit, stood a vertical, three-foot high, heavy tree stump. Fred saw that the top of each stump had a u-shaped notch . . . as if for some kind of barbecue.

It was then that he began struggling violently against his chained wrists and ankles. He quickly realized that it was useless and panicked. He began screaming hysterically as the drums grew suddenly louder and the natives became more excited. They began chanting loudly as if to drown out Fred's piercing screams.

The children stopped chasing each other, and wandered over. They encircled Fred, giggling, fascinated by his writhing and screaming. For a few moments Wagambutti stood quietly looking down at him. He slapped a machete-sized knife against his right thigh while keeping time with the throbbing drums. Then he knelt down beside Fred and spoke in a gentle voice.

"In the distant past, they would cook you slowly while you were still alive. The missionaries taught us less cruel ways. We are now a gentle, more caring people. You will suffer for a very brief time," Wagambutti assured him.

Fred stiffened before squeezing his eyes tightly closed. Wagambutti kept his word to his new found friend. And after a few, short, agonizing minutes . . . Fred's once in lifetime, Island adventure was over.